JIHAD

The Struggle
Within
The Forgiveness of
Sins

H. Courtney Williams
Aka Bilal Abdul Khaaliq

authorHOUSE®

AuthorHouse™
1663 Liberty Drive
Bloomington, IN 47403
www.authorhouse.com
Phone: 833-262-8899

Published by AuthorHouse 10/24/2023

ISBN: 979-8-8230-0887-7 (sc)
ISBN: 979-8-8230-0886-0 (e)

Library of Congress Control Number: 2023910203

Print information available on the last page.

This book is printed on acid-free paper.

Disclaimer

Certain long-standing institutions and agencies are mentioned in this book, but the characters involved are imaginary. Although its form is a memoir, the opinions expressed about religions, institutions, and groups are those of the characters and should not be confused with the authors'. Some passages in this book are actual experiences of the author that have been enhanced for entertainment. Any names or persons resembling any of the characters in this book are purely coincidental.

Book cover illustrated by Twelvv Ramos

CONTENTS

JAIL

I've met guys who've killed their wives.
I've met guys who've killed for fun.
I've met stickup kids and burglars,
and children caught with guns.
I've met guys doing time,
who were caught while on the run.
I've met guys who've committed crimes
and are doing time for fun.
Misdemeanors, felonies, probation and parole,
all these words are new to me,
I want no part of them at all.
I just want to get back home
in one piece and do my time,
and never see this place again
or commit another crime.

by H. Courtney Williams

CHAPTER 1

The Road to Hell

"Be patient! You're a man. You're a Muslim," was an oath I made the very first time the reality of imprisonment overwhelmed my thoughts, when the painful anguish of solitary confinement was all that was left to living. Death by suicide was not an option. There would be a heavy punishment in the Hereafter for anyone who traveled that route, and to escape from one hell only to find oneself engulfed by eternal damnation for committing this major offence against God, was not worth the trade-off. The virtue, patience, is what I practiced to maintain my sanity. "In God's time, in God's time," I would say to myself repeatedly until my anxiety subsided.

As I uncovered my face only moments after waking, the cold air in this dimly lit room, which was now my permanent residence, was filled with the sounds of rattling window sashes, howling winds and the rustling leafless branches of winter weathered trees. I was an avid outdoorsman, who had spent many a bone-chilling night under the cover of northern New York's darkest skies and had never seen a night the likes of this in early spring. Pausing momentarily to listen to the havoc Mother Nature was wreaking on all God's creatures that weren't indoors, left me with the feeling that I was somewhat fortunate not to have ever experienced, a night like this in the woods. I arose from my bunk and draped my state issued, green winter jacket over my shoulders, then sat staring in a daze at the window to my cubicle only four feet in front of me. It was the type of daze some do upon awakening after sleep or a long nap. Conscious of this fact, I was still unwilling to snap out of it. It was a comforting feeling, and in jail there are few times when you are at peace with yourself. Relishing in this serene inner calmness, my eyes caught a glimpse of the minute movement of the rattling window before me. *I know I saw it move*, I thought. For some reason at that moment, I felt it was more important to leave my comfort zone and finally snap out of it. Now focusing on the window and awaiting another gale-force wind, there came a howling gust.

There, I knew I saw it move. Oh well, I thought, *that and a box of Oreo cookies won't get me on the go-back bus* (vehicle used to transport inmates, usually to and from court while incarcerated). For some reason though, it made me feel secure, in that I was still on top of things in my environment. As a child, I remember first hearing the phrase *always watch your back* and now in jail that saying had more relevance than apple pie and Chevrolets have to America.

"April?" I questioned myself aloud.

It came as a surprise to me to be experiencing harsh, winter weather conditions in the middle of April. It was spring. Although I had an extensive outdoor background, I was a city boy who used northern New York's woods year-round for recreational purposes only. Hunting, fishing and weekend retreats is how I spent most of my time in the wilds. I had never lived through the full gamut of weather conditions of a sub-Canadian winter until now, less than one hundred miles south of the border, living as a prisoner, at this "medium security" camp called Mohawk.

"Good morning, *akhi!*"

Akhi (ah-kee) is brother in Arabic. Muslim men refer to each other as *akhi* or *akh* (ah-kuh) and all inmates including non-Muslims eventually become aware of the term).

As I turned toward my contradictory greeter, "*Walaikum,*" I responded, "what's up?"

"Who's April, your wife?" he asked.

"No!" I chuckled.

"Oh, you Muslims dream about women too, huh?"

"No, April like the month is what I meant, and it sounds like the dead of winter out there," I said.

"Yeah, that fucking wind kept me up all night," he said.

"All night? What time is it now?" I asked.

"Uhm, 4:35," he replied.

"You'd better be getting ready, *akh,*" he said while looking at his watch.

"Yeah, how's the water, hot?" I asked, referring to the showers.

"Yeah, but you know how it don't last long on cold days like this, and God forbid, excuse me *akh*, I mean

3

Allah forbid, you wind up at the back of the line and gotta take a cold one," he said.

"Yeah, you're right," I said.

"Ok *akh*, I'm gonna see if I can get a little shut-eye before daybreak," he said.

"Yeah, you do that," I said. With that, he turned and stepped into his cubicle next to mine.

"*Asalaamu alaikum*," he said.

"*Walaikum salaam*," I responded.

"Hey *akh*, what's that mean anyway?" he asked.

At that point, I lowered my head and smiled. It was always a pleasure for me to discuss religion, especially my religion or way of life, Islam, to anyone who showed true interest.

"Weren't you taught never to use big words that you didn't understand?" I asked.

"Yeah," he responded, with a dumbfounded smile.

"It means *may Allah's peace be upon you*," I said.

"Wow, that's some deep shit, *akh*. You Muslins be really deep man. I always wanted to talk to a Muslim about Allah and shit. Damn, excuse me, *akh*. I fucked up again. I'm sorry man, no disrespect," he said apologetically.

"Yeah, old habits are hard to break. Allah knows what's in your heart," I said.

"You know…" he started, "I don't even know if I believe in God anymore."

"Did you ever?" I asked.

"Yeah, I thought I did, up till my little brother got pushed off a roof in the Bronx the same year my father blew his brains out." Mel paused, then forcibly inhaled deeply, then exhaled and continued in a somber voice.

"My mother, before she died, used to read the Bible to me and my brother Tommy every night after she tucked us in. She was real religious. Man, I remember her whipping my ass and reciting psalms and verses and shit from the Bible at the same time. She was a good Christian and a damn good mother. She was just fucked up on that shit. They found her nude body in Edgecombe Park, Uptown, Sugar Hill, around the corner from my house with her pantyhose knotted around her neck. Shit was embarrassing too, for the whole damn neighborhood to be looking at your moms with no clothes on, strapped up with a spike in her arm. It's funny though, sometimes I'd get into fights because somebody would call my moms a hoe, teasing me and shit. But after that shit in the park, nobody ever fucked with me like that again. I was only nine years old, but I remember that shit like it was yesterday."

He continued with, "Right then and there, while I was looking at my father trying to break loose from the cops. He was just trying to get closer to my mother's body, but that was the first time I ever questioned if there was a God or not. I just couldn't see how a real God would allow some shit like that to happen to somebody who believed in him as much as my moms did. I prayed that night for the first time on my own without my moms having to tell me to. I didn't remember all the words to the *Our Father* and *The Hail Mary*, but me and my brother Tommy kept saying them over and over till my pops made us stop to go to bed. After he cut the lights out, we got back outta bed and we tried to pray till daybreak. I kept waking Tommy up and telling him we gotta pray mommy into Heaven. But I fell asleep too, and in the morning, I woke up while my pops was putting us back in the bed. And then when I was seventeen, my pops and my brother…" At that point Mel paused and took a deep breath.

"You alright?" I asked.

"Yeah *akh*, my life's just been so fucked up man. I don't know what to believe anymore," he said.

"Believe this," I said, "There is a God and Allah is the best of planners. This is His world; we're just living in it. Our aim is to get to Heaven by His rules, not ours and no matter how tragic the circumstances, he wouldn't make us carry a burden heavier than we can bear."

"Who is Allah, *akh*?"

"Allah is who you refer to as God," I said."

"Then why don't you just call Him God?" he asked.

"Good question," I said. "See, the Old English word God comes from the Proto-Germanic language that originated in Northern Europe around 500 BC. That's 500 years before Christ. In the Mid-East, even Arab-Christians use the proper noun Allah in reference to God as the Holy Trinity… In Arabic, the word God is Allah. To be more precise, in Arabic the word *Al* means *the* and when joined with *lah* (Al-lah), they mean *The God*. We believe there are no partners as in the Holy Trinity. God the Father is God to a Muslim, and we do believe in Jesus…

"Damn you Muslims are smart," he said.

"No, just inquisitive. And don't ask me what that means," I said jokingly.

"Oh, I know what quizitive means. That's something you do during a test in school," he said then he burst into laughter at his own dim wit.

"Shhhh!" echoed through the dorm by inmates who were trying to sleep.

"You'd better sit down before you get hit with a battery or something," I said.

"One of them niggas hit me with some shit, it'll be the last thing they throw," he said loudly in a threatening tone of voice.

Just then, from across this small four-man room, which was actually an extension of this fifty-five-man dormitory that my dormmates called the *penthouse* came, "*Ay Dios Mio, silencio por favor!*" It was grumbled by Rico, one of its four residents as he whipped back his blanket and abruptly sat up.

"Hey, I'm sorry man," said Mel, as Rico angrily shuffled off to the lavatory, bare-chested and dragging the heels of his slippers loudly. Born Miguel Sanchez, Rico immigrated to the South Bronx, New York in his early thirties from Dos Bocas, a small village just south of the coastal town Arecibo in Puerto Rico. It was on the mean streets of the Bronx where he acquired his nickname shortly after his arrival.

"Well, it's getting late," I said. "Let me hit the showers while the water's still hot."

After Mel sat on his bunk, he laid back and said, "Hey *akh.*"

"Yeah."

"Do you think my moms went to Heaven, man?" he asked.

"That'll be between her and Allah come judgement day. What if we continued this conversation after *chow*?" I said.

"Yeah *akhi*, thanks man," he said.

Melvin Turner was a twenty-eight-year-old Manhattan born father of two, just coming down off a fifteen-year bid of which he served eight years for the attempted murders of his wife and the neighborhood drug dealer he happened to find in his bed one day when he came home early from work. Some nights we, his dorm-mates, were awakened by "I'll kill you bitch! I'll kill you bitch!" being screamed repeatedly until someone shook his rack. We had short conversations in the past. Mostly pertaining to the conditions at Mohawk, but never had we conversed theologically.

Mel and I had been neighbors for the past month, and he pretty much knew my daily routine, in as much as I would wake, shower and make *Fajr* (morning prayer). This was one of five obligatory prayers Muslims make daily. He was also a current substance abuser and could be found awake at any given hour during the night, on any given night of the week. I was a recovering addict who had only two and a half years of sobriety and although heroin, cocaine and marijuana were easily accessible, I had reached my lowest ebb in life or hit bottom through my reckless overindulgence before coming to prison. I was trying to get home, not trying to get high.

Mel's family history seemed to be stereotypical of many career criminals I've met in the past. But unlike a *predicate* (career criminal), he was genuinely a good kid growing up, but as a young man he had made the mistake of experimenting with drugs and seemed to have married a substance abusing woman who had led him to believe it was him and not his weekly paycheck that she was truly interested in.

From what I gathered in the short conversations we had as neighbors, this was his first arrest and conviction. He had loved his wife and one-year-old son deeply. His wife was five months pregnant with his now seven-year-old daughter on the day he tried to take her life. He explained in his own words, "I walked in. I saw red and I lost it."

Typical of many young men behind bars, Mel got caught up in the use and trafficking of drugs on the inside. Him being a user before coming to jail, compounded by the many bad hands that life had dealt him, made it not too hard to understand how this good kid had come to jail and gone astray.

I had been lucky enough to leisurely shower with constant hot water and make morning prayer. The howling winds had subsided and now lying on my bunk, I could hear every so often, the rustle of the branches of the old maple tree that was just beyond my window. It was well past dawn and the daylight coming in the window made for good reading of my Quran, which was also part of my daily routine. I always liked to get in a good hour of reading before *chow*. Then suddenly, my nose caught the distinct aroma of top-grade marijuana smoke. Being an ex-addict and marijuana having been my favorite drug of choice, I instinctively inhaled through my nose to my lung's capacity. I was wistfully reminiscing younger days where gathered friends futilely competed at guessing its national origin by the smell. Then just as suddenly, my surroundings told me something was wrong with this picture. Jail and drugs do not mix.

I had acquired a detrimental appreciation for its rank, sweet smell, but my first and foremost objective at this moment was to clear the air A.S.A.P...I leaped from my bunk, and in an instant, I was at the window to my cubicle. After opening it wide, I turned to see Mel fast asleep with a joint still burning between his thumb and index finger. I reached over the low partition that separated us and slapped him on the inside of his right foot. He opened his eyes briefly and when they slowly began to close, I grabbed his right ankle firmly, shook hard one time, then continued to apply pressure until I was sure he was coherent. His eyes focused on mine.

"Hey *akh*," he said, while still holding the joint.

"You plan on putting that out, or are you holding it for one of these cops to take a hit?" I said facetiously.

He then reached up while still lying fully clothed and, on his back, held the still smoldering joint over the ashtray at the edge of his locker, and dropped it, lit, on top of the many hand-rolled cigarette butts that he had accumulated during the night. Then he slowly closed his eyes and began to snore. *This guy's trouble*, I thought to myself... All jails have a Peter pays for Paul policy. Meaning, if Paul gets caught doing wrong, Peter, and all his brothers I might add, will pay. I reached across to his locker and picked up the ash tray, then took the joint and flicked it through the bars of my window. There were three small containers of milk on the sill that I had placed there the day before. I sometimes used my sill as a means of keeping things cold, such as milks and juices.

Suddenly, "Freeze, Eighteen!" was shouted by the CO on duty.

He had smelled the marijuana smoke and had come to investigate. I wasn't concerned so much as to be blamed for smoking reefer, as I was for just the mere confrontation with one of these wanna-be state troopers. I was a good liar, as my many years of drug abuse had somehow affected that craft and knew this guy's departmental interrogation tactics were no match for my well-honed evasive techniques based on street knowledge. To put it simply, I was an ex-addict, and he was, well, a country boy.

"Didn't I say freeze?"

As he repeated the order, with blatant insubordination, I reached for one of the containers, and put it, and the ashtray on my locker. Then I turned and sat on my bunk.

"On your feet, Eighteen!" was the next order shouted by the now red-faced CO, who at this point was standing in my cube and looking down at me as if I were his property and he was my slave master. All cubicles are numbered and eighteen was mine. They sometimes used this number at mail call, and although reluctantly at first, you eventually respond to it as if it were your given name.

"Get up, boy!" was the next command, and the cracker in him showed.

"What did you call me?" I asked in a low and threatening tone while rising from my bunk. Instinctively I stepped toward him in a threatening posture.

I paused when he stepped back and blurted out, "I told you to freeze two times. You disobeyed a direct order two times. Where's that shit you been smoking?"

"In my ashtray," I said angrily.

"Give it here," he demanded.

I handed him the ashtray.

"Which one of these butts is marijuana?" he asked.

"What?" I retorted.

"Oh, you're gonna be a problem, huh?" he said.

"Look," I said, "if you refer to me again by anything other than my name or my number, you will have a problem with me. Now what's your problem?" I asked.

"Oh yeah, oh yeah?" he repeated, "We'll just see about that. Up against the wall, you know the routine," he said. And in the next instant, he was on his walkie-talkie calling for back-up.

I was making a conscious effort to stall and distract this officer long enough for Mel to clean up his act and get rid of any evidence. From the position I was in, I could not see if Mel had awakened from all the commotion. Knowing from past experiences in a situation such as this, all contraband had better be well hidden or gotten rid of. Evidence of drugs or weapons equaled shake down and possession of either equaled box time, and no one wanted to go to jail, in jail.

I was hoping Mel had awakened from his deep sleep. He had been up all night and now was no time to be sleeping. After all, if it wasn't for his carelessness and lack of concern for his fellow inmates, we wouldn't be in this precarious situation. A shake down would take all morning, and by the time you picked up all of your belongings from the center of the floor and put them back to where you previously had them, it would be lunch time and most of us were hungry for breakfast.

As I stood spread eagle against the wall in my cube,

I watched through my window as the sun played a game of peek-a-boo from behind the clouds that now seemed to threaten a no-show appearance of its daily act. Then in the distance behind me, I heard the sound of at least three pairs of running boots and the unmistakable sound of jailer's keys, of which each officer had his own private set. Now my attention turned to my personal safety. I knew how much these farm-raised wannabes liked to make an example of minority city boys like me, and how they meted out punishment to any inmate who they judged deserving of it.

Then from the corner of my eye, I thought I saw Mel rise from his bunk, and was sure of it when I heard him in an abnormally loud voice greet me with, "*Assalamu alaikum.*"

As I turned my head, "*Walaikum salaam*," I responded.

I could see Mel was behind the first CO and using himself as a human shield acting as a buffer to hopefully break the stride of the assisting officers in their response to this officer in distress call. He had also used the Islamic greeting loudly, so as to let all of the officers involved know that this was a Muslim affair and they had better ask questions before they hurt an innocent Muslim and had to be responsible for an Islamic uprising. Mel was fully aware of these consequences and knew they applied to inmates and officers alike.

Nationwide, most inmates who are sentenced to *state time* (sentences of one year or more) have been incarcerated long enough to understand the basic rules of Islamic culture behind bars. By the time they've finished their days in court, going back and forth from the county lockup before their sentencing, they would have also experienced the violence and some prison rules of gang culture that permeates these county run hellholes.

"On the lock down!" shouted the first assisting officer as he encountered Mel who had made himself a human obstacle.

Mel slowly turned around, folded his arms, then faced the officer and said, "Excuse me, you're blocking the entrance to my cube."

As the officer stepped to the side, Mel slowly took the two steps to his cube all the while looking the officer in the eyes. It's the eyes that tell the level of a man's adrenalin surge, and these guys looked like savages. As the officer stood motionless with baton in hand, he angrily glared back at Mel. This tactic had worked, and I was still standing unharmed. It was not unusual for an inmate who caused an officer to call for backup to be beaten first and then asked questions. I was lucky.

"Hi Lieutenant," I heard one of the officers say as he greeted an out-of-breath obese officer in a white shirt with lieutenant bars. He was the last to step in. In all, it made a total of four officers who had come to the rescue of one.

"Bilal!" he said, as I turned my head in response to my name.

It was a pleasure to see Lieutenant Nealy, who I knew from a previous acquaintance to distinctly be a kind man. He escorted me to this dorm from the draft room where new inmates fresh off the bus sign in the first day I arrived. That day, he reached out for my hand and said, "Welcome to Mohawk." Then he asked my name and where I locked. After I told him, he told me he was on his way over there also and to grab my belongings and follow him. It saved me about three hours of waiting around for an escort. I was wearing my *kufi* (a short, brimless, rounded cap worn by Muslim men), and he said, "Of all the inmates, I like Muslims because they aren't troublemakers." I was surprised he remembered my name and this was the first I've seen him since.

"Hey Lieutenant! How you doin?" I asked.

"What's the problem?" he asked back.

It was not customary procedure to ask an inmate the details of a situation before asking a fellow officer.

"I don't know. I opened the window to air this place out cause I left a cigarette burning in my ashtray. It had the whole place stinking, and I didn't want the rest of the guys to have to smell it. Then this guy comes in talking about, *Freeze!* At first, I thought he was talking about how cold I was making it back here with the window up. He sounded like he was accusing me of smoking reefer, then he called me a boy. He wouldn't call me that in New York," I said angrily, referring to the city.

"Oh yeah?" said the first CO. "What's that milk doing on the windowsill? You just bought yourself a slug, son," and pulled out his pad and started to write me a ticket for having milk outside of my window.

By now the scent of marijuana was completely gone and my story had even convinced the complaining officer, to the point where there was no more questioning in reference to the original marijuana accusation. While he was writing the ticket, Lieutenant Nealy stood directly in front of him, looking down his nose with both hands in his pockets, complete with a look of distain.

When the officer finished writing, before he could look up, Lieutenant Nealy plucked the ticket from his hand and told the officers present, "Leave me alone with him."

As the officers exited the room, the assisting officers were playfully harassing the complaining officer with elbow jabs to his ribs and intentional careless baton strikes. In their eyes, he had made a rookie type mistake and they were not going to let him get away with it without reprimand.

"So how do you like Mohawk?" asked Nealy.

"Like it?!" I exclaimed. He realized his question didn't sit well with me.

"You know those milks don't belong out there," he said.

"Yeah, I know. One of my roomies must have placed them out there; they're not mine," I explained as I looked directly at Mel.

At that point, Mel had a look of shock on his face and turned his head then laid back on his bunk. I figured I'd make him sweat a little for all the trouble he caused me.

"Well, just keep your nose clean and don't give these cowboys anything to shoot at if you know what I mean. And as for this," he said while holding up the ticket, "don't worry about it," then ripped it in half and handed it to me.

"Thanks a lot, Lieutenant," I said. Then we shook hands and he walked out.

Most of the guards at this camp were local boys who grew up on chicken and dairy farms. This part on northern New York was known for its production of poultry and dairy products. What was little known by outsiders was that this was Klan country. Nepotism here was routinely practiced by the administration's personnel staff, and you could plainly see the family resemblance on many of the officers' faces. These were sons and nephews of Klansmen, who from a very early age were indoctrinated into the brotherhood. Ignorance flowed fluently amongst these men and intellectualism was met with stiff opposition whenever it presented itself in the form of a Black man.

No sooner than Nealy making his exit, the *AM chow call* was being aired over the intercom, when suddenly Rico bolted from his cubicle which was directly across from Mel's.

He stood in the entrance to Mel's cubicle and shouted, "You watch that shit!" He repeated, "You watch that shit! You almost fuck up everybody. You watch that shit, I'm telling you," while pointing his finger disrespectfully in Mel's face, and speaking with a heavy Puerto Rican accent.

Rico was twice Mel's age and virtually half his size but was in perfect health and in uncommonly good physical shape for a man his age. He had been down for nineteen years and spent all of his spare time in the weight yard consoling and advising his troops. He also had a reputation for being the only one in the yard who didn't wait in line to use equipment. The inmates fondly referred to him also as *Popi* and gave him the utmost respect. He was a real gentleman until someone rubbed him the wrong way and apparently Mel had done that, for the second time that day.

Mel just sat in silence with his head hung low and his hands clasped between his knees.

Rico was mad as hell and continued with, "You bitch ass nigga, we kill you in Green Haven for that shit (Green

17

Haven Correctional Facility, Stormville, NY). You owe *akhi*," he looked at me and said, "He owe you *akhi*, make him pay, he owe you."

Then he glanced disdainfully at Mel and grumbled profanities in Spanish as he turned and walked out for *chow*. Rico was also the undisputed leader of the gang called Neta at Mohawk, a multi-racial group, predominantly Puerto Rican, whose primary function in prisons was to protect one another from unfair treatment by other inmates. They also had other nefarious activities that were typical of gang bangers in jail.

Then, when all the scolding seemed to be over, there came from across the room, the fourth member of our semiprivate quarters, Woody. He walked into Mel's cube, and as Mel looked up at him, Woody palmed Mel's face and mushed him hard.

As Mel rolled back on his bunk, Woody shouted, "Get up, get up motha fucka so I can kick your ass!" Mel just laid there. Woody continued. "You chicken shit motha fuckas are all alike. You walk around this motha fucka like you own it, getting high in public, jeopardizing everybody around you, like we got more time to give to this fucked up system. Up motha fucka!" He shouted once again. "Get up so I can stomp a mud hole in your ass!"

He paused momentarily, and when Mel didn't oblige the challenge. He looked at me and said, "Popi's right. He owes you *akh*, tax this nigga!" He looked back at Mel and said, "Punk ass nigga, let me catch you smoking that shit back here again. I'll break your fuckin' jaw."

Woodrow Collins was doing time for possession of an illegal firearm which he used in self-defense, killing two members of a three-man stick-up team. He was thirty-six years old and had sold drugs all his life. Born in Brooklyn and now a born-again Christian, I overheard him saying in his prayers on numerous occasions how sorry he was for taking human lives and how remorseful he was for destroying so many families. Woody was a prime example of how jail can turn a man around and entice him from *gangsta life* into wanting to conform to society's idea of being a productive citizen. He had graduated high school and attended one year at John Jay College in downtown Manhattan, where he was suspended and never to return due to charges of alleged drug trafficking. His childhood aspiration was to become a lawyer, but his goal fell far short of that once he tasted the bittersweet life in the fast lane of drug peddling. Doing state time in prison, he watched all of his worldly possessions virtually evaporate in front of his eyes. He had become disillusioned by his assets, and the false feeling of security that many drug distributors have as long as they're in possession of their ill found wealth. And like many before and after him, he found himself fearful of the lifestyle that awaited him back on the outside. He worked in the law library and attended college classes in pursuit of his childhood dream. Woody was used to living a very comfortable life on the outside, and decided while in jail, to never again let anything he worked so hard and so long for be so easily taken away, including his good time, which Mel had just so carelessly placed in jeopardy.

"And that ain't a threat, that's a promise," was the last thing Woody said to Mel as he left his cubicle and returned to his own to get his state jacket to leave for *chow*.

After Woody exited, a few moments passed in silence.

I was making the last few adjustments in arranging my cube before I was to leave for *chow* when Mel blurted out, "Oh God, why can't I stop doing these drugs? I just want to get home to my babies."

As he threw himself backwards on his bunk, tears were running down his face and I knew the feeling. Many times over the years during my bout with drug addiction, there were plenty of episodes of me neglecting my family, my responsibilities and myself. It wasn't until I started living by the Laws of God, that I was able to get my addiction and myself under control. Islam guided me through the darkness and the pain and through the profound feeling of hopelessness that every addict lives with while under the captivity of drugs. Mel was caught up in his addiction to the point of being oblivious to the consequences and the world around him, and jail was no place to be living even slightly unaware of your surroundings. It was obvious Mel was an addict in trouble who needed direction and hopefully he would one day find guidance, preferably of a divine nature.

"Mel, God's not going to grant wishes to anyone just for the asking or by broadcasting information over an intercom like they do here, especially if you're doing nothing to please Him," I said.

"What *akhi*?" asked Mel.

"You just asked God why you couldn't stop doing drugs, right?"

"Yeah."

Have you ever done anything more than just ask?" I replied.

"What do you mean, *akh*?"

"Have you prayed?" I asked

"Sometimes," he said.

"Does that mean only when you want something?"

"Yeah, I guess," he said.

"If you've prayed sometimes, I'll assume you believe in God, at least sometimes. Therefore, I'll also assume you believe in the Devil or *Shaiton* (Satan)."

He nodded in agreement.

"Well, it would please the Devil to no end to cause more misery between you, your children and God, and as long as you continue to please him with your selfish ways, he will continue to please himself through you and people like you. Don't you go in front of the board soon?"

"Yeah, *akh*."

"How would it look to them if you walked in there with a slug for possession, in jail?"

Without waiting for his reply, I continued, "You'd be standing there looking dumbfounded when they asked you about it. Then you'd come back in here crying about how you still want to see your babies after they hit you with a nice chunk of what you got on the back of your bid. Meanwhile your babies would be crying, 'When is Daddy coming home?'

Look man, I'm not trying to scream on you, 'cause I've been where you're at. I just want for my brother what I want for myself, understand?"

"Yeah, *akh*. I understand."

"Do you really?" I asked. Mel didn't answer. He continued to lay on his back now with a resolved look on his face. Hopefully there was something in what I said to which he would take heed.

"Going to *chow*?" I asked.

"No *akh*, I'm not hungry. I'm just going to stay here and think about what you said."

"Yeah, here's your ashtray," and he reached up as I handed him the ashtray that I had taken off his locker earlier.

"You losing weight, man. You want these milks?" I asked.

"Yeah *akh*, just leave them on your locker, I'll get them in a minute."

As I was putting on my jacket, I noticed Mel was in deep thought. "Later," I said as I stepped past the entrance to his cubicle. As I stepped out of our semi-private room into the main dorm, I noticed most of the other inmates had already left for *chow*, and it was a signal that if I did not leave now, I would be risking the possibility of being a straggler or late for *chow*.

The morning crew of officers who worked the mess hall had a reputation for harassing latecomers by asking them for their ID cards, strip-searching them and then turning them away to head back to their dorms without eating. *I've got to hurry*, I thought to myself. As I rushed past the CO's desk before exiting the dorm, there he sat with his legs crossed and his feet propped up on the desk.

With hands clasped behind his head, in his most authoritative tone of voice, he said "Slow down before I write you another ticket, for speeding."

"You didn't write me the first one," was my reply, and I never broke stride or pace while ignoring his demand.

He was looking for trouble, but there were no rules against being in a hurry as long as you were not running. Now exiting the dorm and passing through the doorway into the stairwell, the temperature change was noticeable enough to make me immediately aware that I wasn't donning my *kufi*. Oh how I wished I had left it on my locker, so as to remind myself to never forget it, especially on cold days such as this. *I can't pass this chump again without him provoking me to do something that I'll wind up getting a ticket for,* I thought, *if I go back for it, I know I'll be late for chow. And if I don't, I'll be risking catching a cold and possibly wind up not eating anyway.* Between a rock and a hard place seemed to be a bit more comfortable than the situation in which I found myself at the moment. My hunger drove me to continue at the same pace to the top of the stairs. As I approached the entrance door to the building, the whistling sound of rushing air coming from the door was the deciding factor on which I based my decision to skip *chow.* Staring through the door's small window I found myself reminiscing thoughts of the month of fast. It was the month of *Ramadan* (religious holiday for Muslims; a time of self-reflection and to strengthen a relationship with Allah) five weeks earlier. I had just made congregational prayer and broke fast with the *ummat* (Muslim population) which numbered slightly above one hundred.

That evening as we walked back from the mosque in below zero temperatures, someone yelled, "Look!" and pointed to the new moon.

It signified the ending of the month of *Ramadan.* It meant the month of fast was over. It was a sight to behold.

There it hung. Its thin white crescent against a vast royal blue sky, hanging like a pendulum anchored somewhere in God's Heaven. It was through this same window that I stopped to take one last look at the new moon that night before going downstairs to my dorm. As I stared through the doors window, I found myself in a daze such as the one I was in earlier this morning. My eyes were focused on a frozen patch of ice that had formed overnight from a puddle of water caused by a rain storm the previous day. Thoughts of home and family clouded my mind and the profound feeling of loneliness crept up on me as it always did whenever I found myself all alone. *Jail is hell*, was my last thought before into the picture came a speeding van. Its bright yellow and black insignia on the door identified it as a state vehicle. I watched as the vehicle was coming to an abrupt stop. Its right front tire sliding across the pool of ice not spinning until the ice below it fractured and burst into a spray of water and ice.

Before the van came to a halt, one officer leaped from the van's side door and cleared the now shattered pool. After he touched down, he turned and started running full tilt up the pathway to my dorm. Seconds later he was being followed by three more officers including the driver. They were coming towards me like line-backers, and I was the opposing football team. It all seemed surreal at first, somewhat like a silent movie as I backed up clear to the wall behind me. It was all too real when they came crashing through the door, shattering the silence of the small lobby.

"Where's A dorm?" the first officer shouted.

I calmly shook my head implying I didn't know. *Never help the cops. Rule number one.*

"Pauly, come with me. You guys check downstairs," ordered the first officer as he bolted toward the staircase.

As he turned away, I noticed tucked under his right arm was a large white bag. As he started to ascend the staircase, I could clearly see a bright red cross on its side. This was a medical emergency, and these guys were clearly out to save lives, Black or otherwise.

Moments later, "Hey Mack!" was shouted by one of the officers who descended the stairs.

"Yo!" was the response from the top floor. "Down here," came the last call, and the shuffling of feet followed by the slamming of a door signaled that Mack and Pauly were on their way down.

I knew all along where A dorm was. It was my dorm, but like I said, never help the cops. As Mack and the other officer passed by, I immediately took off behind them. As I descended the stairs, I questioned myself as to what could have happened in the short period of time that I was gone. Re-entering the dorm, I saw the CO on duty at his desk with the phone to one ear and his walkie-talkie to the next.

"He's dead, I don't know," I heard him say as I passed his desk now running at full tilt as Mack and Pauly before me.

I saw through the large arched opening of my semi-private quarters, the other two officers moving hastily about in my room. *Mel!* I thought. *He's the only one back there who didn't go to chow.*

"What's going on?" I said to one of the onlooking inmates as I stopped outside the doorway.

"I don't know," he said, "I just woke up to this shit."

As I stepped in, my worst fears were confirmed when I noticed Mel's gray Zodiac running shoes on the feet of the person who was lying in a pool of blood surrounded by Mack's medical team.

"Is he alive?" I asked. No one answered. "Is he alive?" I asked once again, louder this time.

This time between breaths while he was performing mouth to mouth CPR, "Just barely," was reported by Mack.

I noticed a white disposable shaver with the head broken in half, lying on the floor by one of the assisting medical officer's knees and thought to myself, *Why?* I was then overcome by rage, anger stemming from the unjust treatment that went on behind all prison walls. Anger from knowing that this happens every day to frustrated prisoners who check out because they didn't know how to deal with their misfortunes. Angered by the way society sets the trap for underprivileged citizens to continuously wind up in a place like this, and mad at myself for the guilt I felt. If only I hadn't been so harsh. Maybe I should have kept my opinion to myself. If only I had known... I searched my mind for answers until it finally dawned on me, that Allah is the best of planners. The best thing I could do for Mel at this point was pray and ask Allah to spare his life, so I could hopefully one day explain to him how foolish it was to take one's life and the penalty that awaited anyone who did. I turned and rushed to the lavatory where I washed for prayer (*wudu*). Then stopped in the first empty cubicle and started making *salat* (ritual prayer) for the soul of this dying young man. He wasn't a bad kid; in fact, he wasn't a kid at all. He was just a young man with good intentions, the kind of which, the road to hell is paved.

CHAPTER 2

The Dogs

Weeks passed and Mel's condition was updated daily through the grapevine by prisoners who worked in the infirmary. It was a pleasure for me to think that Allah had spared Mel's life and maybe, just maybe, I may have helped, if even just a little.

The weather was changing nicely. Sometimes the temperature soared into the mid-sixties and thoughts of spin casting lures for largemouth bass made me long for freedom. Fishing was my first love and passion and days like these reminded me of how thin patches of ice can form overnight on a lake and be gone an hour after sunrise, allowing me unobstructed access to a weedless lake bottom. This time of year, when the water was just above freezing, made fishing the bottom with a rubber night crawler a very productive way to bring home the big ones. Nearing the end of May, the frosty, cold mornings were just a memory. Now days full of sunshine and warmer temperatures were the norm. I had outside clearance and worked with the outside lawns and grounds crew: the *dream team* of Mohawk, so aptly nicknamed for the benefits and perks that came with being a member. Of the thirteen hundred inmates there, seventeen had outside clearance but only four of us actually worked outside the gate. We, the outside lawns and grounds crew, did the landscaping in the summer and the snow in the winter. There was a record snowfall this year but now cutting grass was our regular routine. It got boring at times, but I'll trade pulling a bushwhacker with a tractor, than pushing a plow with it any day of the year.

Six weeks had passed since Mel *cut up*, a term used by inmates to describe a wrist slashing. *The penthouse* had a new resident, number nineteen, an O-G (old gangster) named Benjamin Watts, a sixty-seven-year-old great grandfather who ran an illegal daily number business in Harlem. He was an old street hustler born in Chicago who took pride in his knowledge of the street and preferred to be called Mr. Watts.

"I got one for you, *akhi*!" he exclaimed one morning as I was reading my Quran, awaiting the *chow call*.

"I thought you fell asleep," I said.

"Now you know Bilal, once I'm up, I'm up," he said

"Yeah, you right. Ok, shoot," I said.

"What year did they take the wheat leaves off the back of the penny?" he asked loudly, as though he were sure he would stump me in a continual game of trivia that started the first day he arrived. It sometimes made for good laughs, and certainly made time pass more quickly.

"Nineteen fifty-nine!" I answered.

"You gotta do better than that," I said and smiled.

"Oooo wee!" he exclaimed, "You hear that, Woody?

Either this boy's really smart or he's just old as hell," he said.

"Damn *akh!*" said Woody. "How old are you?" he asked, while lying on his bunk, as the rest of us were in the small four-man room awaiting *chow*.

"Now you don't have to be that old to remember when they changed the penny," I said with caution as I contemplated my age.

Woody seemed genuinely surprised with my answer, nineteen fifty-nine.

"On the real Bilal, how old are you man?" he asked again with sincerity.

"I'll be forty-six in July," I replied.

"You lying," he said with amazement as he sat up on his bunk.

"How old do you think I am?" I asked.

"I thought I had you by at least two years," he said.

"Two years, huh? That would make me about thirty-five?" I asked.

"Thirty-six" he said.

"Yeah, I could live with that," I responded.

"For real," said Woody, "you're forty-five? Damn you look good for your age."

"I was a union, journeyman wall finisher before coming to jail. Hard work and hard drugs, twenty-nine years of plastering and twenty-nine years of being plastered. I wouldn't exactly call it the winning combination, but it worked for me," I said jokingly.

"You hear that, Mr. Watts? Selling drugs can't be all that bad if it has a preserving effect on the human anatomy," said Woody, knowing that false statement would get a rise out of Watts.

"Now don't you start that shit, trying to justify selling that shit to your own people," he replied. "That God damn devil dust is cursed man. I could'a sold that shit instead of banking numbers, and I remember when the price of that shit was high as giraffe pussy. Now for me, money ain't never been a problem, but my boys was droppin' like flies, and at every card game, you heard about somebody else dying from fucking with that shit. Maybe they put some new shit in that motha fucka that could bring the dead back to life or somethin', but they used to have that shit they called pure shit back in my days. They should'a called it pure hell because hell is what all the people who used it got from fuckin' with that shit," Watts paused. "Shit," he stated with a hint of disappointment in his voice, "we used to take up collections at every card game for dumb niggas that would drop dead who was fool enough to try that shit."

Watts continued, "Man, after all these years, I still got niggas widows coming by my spot. Old bitties I give a little handout to every now and then. Some of 'em got some real good pussy too, like Mabel, Big Charlie's wife. He used to hold floating card games in Harlem or the Bronx every weekend and Mabel and her girls used to give them dances at the Renaissance and the Audubon Ballroom. Mabel gave a gig one time at Smalls Paradise on 135th and 7th. That's where I met my first wife, God bless her soul. Man, those were the days, but y'all young boys wouldn't know nothin' 'bout 'dat der. All's I can say, is anybody who's fool enough to fuck with that dope is a dope and

31

deserves everything they gits and that goes for buying it or selling it."

"Mr. Watts," chuckled Woody, he was still in the let's crank-up Mr. Watts mode, "I ain't talkin' bout heroin, I'm talkin' cocaine man!"

Watts replied, "It's all the same shit, drugs is drugs. Now, if a nigga wants to get high all's he gotsta do is walk to the corner and buy a bottle of fine scotch, like Johnnie Black or some Courvoisier cognac." Watts paused again. "Damn, I could use a drink right now!" he exclaimed. "Damn, y'all done kicked my shit up now. I wish they'd hurry up and call *chow*, goddamn."

"Hey Mr. Watts," I said, "what's the name of the building that they replaced those wheat leaves with?"

Watts thought for a moment. "Oh, that'd be the Capital, son," he replied.

"The Capital!" exclaimed Woody, then he burst into uncontrollable laughter.

"What the hell's wrong wit you, boy?" said Watts.

When Woody finally stopped laughing, he said, "Tell 'em *akh*."

"The Lincoln Memorial," I replied in a low voice, while smiling from the humor of it all.

Then, to make matters worse, Rico stood up, looked over the partition to his cube, which was directly opposite Mr. Watts' and said, "Everybody know that Benjie."

Mr. Watts had no problem with Rico calling him Benjie, understanding that he spoke broken English and all, except on occasion.

"Oh shut up and sit down, and my name ain't no goddamn Benjie...Where's my damn cigarettes?" he grumbled as he rose from his bunk and opened his locker, scattering his belongings carelessly about.

"You let these niggas in the country and automatically overnight they's goddamn geniuses. What you in here for anyway?" he snapped, as he stopped and looked directly at Rico.

"Selling dope!" replied Rico and smiled.

"See, there's another dummy going to hell in a hand basket," said Watts.

At that point Woody burst into laughter, this time rolling back on his bunk holding his stomach as the *chow* bell sounded. Woody's laugh was contagious, it always brought a smile to my face. As I stood up, I noticed Rico looking at Woody with a devilish grin. They got a kick out of rousing Mr. Watts' temper and took advantage of every opportunity to have a few clean laughs. I must admit that I've been known to instigate a few hearty bellows of laughter at the expense of Mr. Watts' temper myself at times.

As I exited the building on my way to *chow*, I noticed it was a beautiful day. The temperature was in the mid-fifties and there wasn't a cloud to be seen in the sky.

"Hey Bilal, over here!" shouted Abdul Alim (Al-leem), one of my Muslim brothers with whom I ate *AM* and *PM* *chow* every day. He locked in E dorm on the third floor and whoever exited the building first, would slow-walk until the other came out and caught up.

Upon my approach, "*Assalamu alaikum*" he greeted.

"*Walaikum salaam*," I replied.

"We didn't get no sleep upstairs last night," he said.

"Why, what happened?"

"These two *kafirs* (non-believers) started arguing over the TV. You know that boy James who goes with that homo named Queen Mother?"

"Yeah."

"Well, him and this other fool who just transferred-in yesterday, got into it during the ten o'clock news. This new Spanish kid just up from *the rock* (Rikers Island Correctional Facility) come in there like he trying to run the TV, flippin' the channel all the time, and anytime somebody say something' to him, he try to extort somethin' from 'em. He's a big dude and was probably running the TV or the phones back on the island. The guys in the dorm came to me last night before it happened and asked me, since I'm dorm rep, if the Muslim brothers in the dorm would back 'em up cause this guy's a Latin King. I told him, we ain't gonna start no war over no damn TV, but I'll call a house meeting in the morning after *chow*. These guys were gonna jump him in the showers. I told them to chill. Anyway, I had just walked in the TV room to watch the news like we always do at ten o'clock, and I see James turn to the news and sits down. This big fool gets up and stomps him in the chest and James fell over backwards with the chair. Apparently, they had words, and this started before I got there. The guard hears the commotion and comes in and asks, 'What happened?' And you know nobody said nothin', but James walked out. I watched him go to his cube, and I knew he was strapped when he came back, but he did it so fast, nobody else even suspected it. I walked out and told one of our brothers to tell our boys to make sure their steel was in a safe place, 'cause we might be havin' a shakedown. And sho-nuff man, I got back to the TV room just as this big kid was comin' through the door on his knees. James had his foot up this boy's ass and had him leaking bad. It seemed like every po-leece in the facility was there in less than three minutes wearing hats and bats. Brother, they turned our house upside down and had us standing assholes and elbows, you know, nuts-to-butts naked till after three this morning."

"What'd they get?" I asked, referring to the police's take.

"We needed a good house cleaning 'cause all the Kings was strapped. They all had shanks and bangers. One guy had a whole pack of New York razors, you know, single edged. Don't ask me how he got 'em in. Anyway, they took six guys to the box and got the rest of the house on cube restriction, but they let us out to eat, instead of bringing in our food. Man, I be glad when this bid is over. I'm tired of this jail," said Alim.

"Tired ain't the word. Fed up is more like it. That's the fourth stabbing this month. We averaging one a week and it ain't even summer yet," I said.

"Yeah man," said Alim, "The higher the temperature, the higher the tension in this jail. Last year, by the end of the summer we had thirteen. Five of 'em died for sure right out here on the walkway. This walkway is notorious for hits."

Then he pointed to a guard post, just one of only three that dotted the entire length of this right-turn-here, left-turn-there walkway.

"See the distance between this guard post and the next one (which was approximately one hundred yards away at the next turn)? Well, with a thousand people between 'em, all wearing green, somebody's mama could get raped out here, and the police couldn't ID nobody. I don't even know why they bothered to put 'em up, all they are is decoration for the suits and the brass that come around every few years for the jail's recertification. Oh, and for the guards to get some sleep between movements."

"Man, you need some sleep bad. I was here last year; I know what this walkway is about." I replied.

"Oh man! I must be losing it," he said. "I'm sorry Bilal, I guess being house captain must be getting to me, explaining everything to the new jacks."

I was pretty hungry and thinking about what was instore for us at breakfast, "Man, if I eat another bowl of those wood chips, I'ma turn into a beaver," I said. "How can they call that stuff bran flakes? They got a lotta nerve," I added.

"It keeps the taxpayers happy," said Alim, "The state buys the cheapest products on the market, and what they don't buy, they have us make. Like these state greens and these boots, there're all made by inmates who…"

"Alim!" I said in a stern voice, interrupting him before he started to ramble.

"I was going off again, wasn't I?" he said.

"Man, you funny when you tired," I said.

"*Assalamu alaikum*," we were greeted from behind.

"*Walaikum salaam*," Alim and I responded, as we turned to see an approaching Muslim named Musa.

"Yo-yo," he said with a broad smile on his face. "I got a date. I'm outta here on the fifth of next month."

"*Alhamdulillah*, get down my brother. I'm happy for you," I said.

"See," said Alim, "I told you, you would make the board," referring to parole.

Musa occasionally ate at the same table as Alim and me and had gone in front of the parole board two days earlier.

Musa continued with, "Yesterday after *PM chow*, the mail was already in the house, so after the count they started mail call. I ain't got a letter in three years, so I paid it no mind. I laid down on my bunk and started to read my book and all of a sudden, I hear these guys screaming my name and the CO calls me on the intercom. I jumped up and looked towards the desk and I see everybody looking at me with these funny looks on their faces. The CO got a letter he's waiving at me, and shouts, 'Board!' I forgot all about my reply. Man, I was so scared to open it my hands were shaking. I had to ask the brother in the next cube to open it and read it for me. So I'm reading his face, and the brother started smilin' real hard, then he looked up at me and said, 'Pack up, you outta here!' Man, I ain't gawn lie. I sat down on my bunk, held on to that letter and cried like a baby. Then I made *salat* and thanked Allah for this whole experience. It truly made me a better man. It's hard to believe I'm going home."

"Whatchu got on the back?" I asked.

"Five more on parole," he said.

"That's a long time to stay out of trouble," said Alim.

"Man, I can do this," said Musa, "They ain't never gonna see me again. I'll never own another gun in my life."

"Never say never. I'll give up my guns when they pry my cold dead fingers from the barrel," I said with a smile.

"Bilal! You're a Muslim now, your robbing days are over," Alim said with a hint of disappointment in his voice.

"I was a Muslim before I came to jail, and I used guns to kill paper. I used to shoot competition for the Harlem Hell Fighters Reserve Rifle Pistol Team, at the 369th Armory on 142nd St and 5th Avenue. But that was years ago. Today I need them for people like Brother Musa here," I said with a laugh, while putting one arm over Musa's shoulder and momentarily holding him in a pretend headlock as if to reprimand him for his past ill deeds.

As we walked toward the mess hall at a leisurely pace, we were greeted by other inmates both Muslim and non-Muslim alike, who were on their way back to their dorms from *chow*. The mornings up north just after sunrise were to be appreciated no matter what time of year it was. Being from the city and wanting to lead a rural lifestyle at some point in my life, I took every opportunity to take in the natural beauty of it all. I paid particular attention to sounds and actions of the native wildlife and the daily changes of the weather.

"You know, this place wouldn't be so bad if you took away the buildings and made all this barbed wire disappear," I said.

"You buggin', Bilal?" said Musa. He continued with, "I can't wait to get back to New York. I can't wait to smell the funk of the city and get away from all these mountains."

"I've had enough of these Kings. I wish I could make them disappear," mumbled Alim.

"Kings?" said Musa.

"What's up with that?" he asked.

"Man, they just troublemakers. I'm tired of all their crap. I ain't get no sleep last night, 'cause'a them. They got my house on restriction and I don't know when I'ma get rec again."

"Restriction? For what?" asked Musa.

Alim hesitated, and when he didn't reply, I looked directly at him to see that he was uncharacteristically not fully aware. He was overcome by a lack of sleep, and Musa's question as to why his dorm was on restriction had completely gone right by him.

"Alim! Wake up man," I said, "The brother asked you a question."

"Huh?" he said.

"Restriction," repeated Musa, "why you on restriction? And what the Kings got to do with it?"

The mere mention of the name of any gang brought about an attentive response, and the name Latin King brought on a particular response of concern. By sheer numbers they are the largest gang in the northeast. Gang activity in and outside of jail and members ranging from inmates to correction officers who work in the NYC lockups, such as The Tombs, The Bronx House of Detention, Brooklyn House and Rikers Island, make them an extremely formidable and dangerous group.

"Aw man, them *kafirs* got busted last night in my dorm. One dude tried to start runnin' the TV like he was back on the island and got laced, and his boys didn't have time to stash their weapons before the police got to 'em. They claimin' the rest of the house had to know they were strapped, so they makin' everybody take the weight," said Alim.

"Did they get that sword that you made last year?" asked Musa.

"Am I in the box? answered Alim sarcastically then smiled.

In jails across the country, a large percentage of inmates own weapons. The vast majority of these weapons are stashed within eight feet of its owner, in their sleeping quarters. Weapons in jail are the common denominator of the weak, the strong, the good and the bad. Even a scared weakling could drive home a small piece of steel that would render the largest of men, a stiff lifeless corpse on a cold metal table. The power of steel or metal in jail can change the status of a person, from a zero to a hero or vice versa, or can be traded for other contraband such as drugs or money or for items of clothing or commissary. Gang warfare seems to always be at an all-time high and groups like the Latin Kings, the Netas, the Jamaican Posse, the Bloods, the Crips and the Aryan Brotherhood to name a few, dominate the population of inmates in the northeastern sector of the US, which tends to make the possession of a weapon an equalizing alternative, if not a necessity.

The practice of Islamic lifestyle or being a Muslim should be the same in or out of jail. With it comes the inherent responsibility to protect one another and the weak or helpless from harm and unfair treatment. "The Muslims" are the largest organized group of inmates nationwide. They have been known to attempt to settle a conflict when all others seem to turn their heads or won't lift a hand to help someone being abused or oppressed. Regardless of the odds or physical danger to themselves, it is their obligation to God and mankind to keep the peace, even if they must resort to violence to do so. It is for reasons like these, that some correction officers, for the most part who happen to be Christian in their belief, tend to look at the Muslim population behind bars as just another gang.

As we approached the mess hall, I couldn't help but notice how beautiful the landscape that surrounded the prison compound truly was. Closer and to the north and east rose the Adirondacks with their sharper and higher peaks, some of which were not visible for they were engulfed by the thick, white cumulus clouds that formed from the moisture that rose from Lake Ontario. Off in the distance and to the south and east, were the older and more rounded hills of the Catskills, both of which are part of the Appalachian system of mountain ranges. They border the eastern US and Canada and run from southern Quebec south to the state of Alabama. Some days seemed to be glorious, with the elements combined to a perfect pitch conducive to the comfort of man.

It's good to be alive, I thought, *to witness this great act of beauty and splendor created by an all merciful and all forgiving God.* I pondered, *Why did He somehow manage to allow a wretch like me to partake in the enjoyment of His creations, or least of all to even witness the grandeur of His work?*

A far cry from the city, the term *up north*, to most city dwellers in New York, conceivably brings to mind one thing: jail…The five boroughs of New York City were spared the profound scarring of the earth's surface by the glaciers formed during the Ice Age. A large percentage of native New Yorkers born and raised in New York City have no conception of the vastness of their home state and the natural beauty consisting of mountains, forests and lakes that lie within it. The terms *up north*, *upstate*, and *up the river* – the Hudson River to be exact – are all synonymous when used in reference to prison by some New Yorkers. Because of the virtual lack of variable elevation and overpopulation in the states southeastern most corner, which is New York City and Long Island, city dwellers are somewhat deprived of the natural beauty and the outdoor activities that the state, which is the namesake of their city, has to offer.

Entering the mess hall, passing two guards, one of which wearing kidskin leather gloves with the fingers cut off, reminded me of the Rikers Island Turtles, the guards on Rikers Island who respond to a red alert: an emergency that's defined by a series of flashing red lights located at various points in the corridors. These specially chosen few who seemingly like violence, do double duty as regular correction officers until a red alert is in effect. At that point, they respond in padded vests, riot helmets and batons or hats and bats as the inmates refer to them. Some of these men wear leather gloves to protect their knuckles from inmates' teeth. Seeing this guard or any on-duty correction or police officer with leather gloves, when it's not cold, tells me he's looking for trouble.

"Shake your asses," he cried out as he repeatedly swung his arms out to his sides and punched his palm upon their return.

He was implying for the inmates move quickly.

"One day, somebody's gonna fuck him up," stated a young man behind us.

We had only passed the guard about ten feet back.

"You. Come here!" said the guard, in a loud voice, while the crowded line was still moving forward. He had overheard him. "Hey you!" he shouted. As everyone turned to look, he was pointing at the young man. "Come here!" he yelled angrily.

"What?" responded the young man as if he couldn't imagine what he was being summoned for.

As the young man approached, "What did you say!?" the guard yelled in his face.

"Man, get outta my face, your breath stinks," he said with an attitude. The young man obviously had no fear of the guard.

"Gimme your card," he demanded, referring to his inmate picture ID card that must be kept on your person at all times, even in the dorms.

The young man hesitated, cocked his head to one side, looked back and smiled at the crowd that was piling up quickly. He looked back at the officer with a frown, reached in his back pocket and handed him his card. The instant the officer's fingers touched it, the young man released it so it would intentionally fall to the ground.

"Pick it up," the officer demanded in a bullyish tone of voice. And the young man slowly reached down and slowly held the card out. "On the fuckin' wall and spread 'em, you little bastard," he indignantly demanded.

"Why? What I do?"

"You didn't learn respect. You ain't in New York City now," he replied.

The response to that statement brought about a low rumble of voices from the crowd. These were all city boys, and they didn't like what they heard. The other officer by now had stepped toward the crowd.

"Keep movin', keep it movin'. This ain't a sideshow," he ordered, "Let's go I said," he directed to a small group of onlookers who had completely stopped walking.

"Officer, tell me, what I do?" demanded the young man again.

The officer giving directions then turned around, walked up behind him and said, "You heard him, on the fucking wall."

Simultaneously shoving the young man from behind, the gloved officer stuck his foot out and tripped him so as to cause him to stumble and fall face first into the brick wall of the mess hall. It was done so smoothly that a child could detect that it had been rehearsed to the point of perfection.

"Did you see that?" said Alim.

"Oh, you awake now?" said Musa jokingly.

As the young man sat crouched on the ground holding his mouth with both hands, blood trickled between his fingers and down his chin. He removed his hands from his mouth, looked in his palms and spit out what seemed at first to be a Tic Tac mint in one of them. When he looked up you could see that his incisor teeth had gone completely through his upper lip, and what was left of them, was still showing and hooked through the flesh. Without saying a word, he jumped to his feet and charged the officers swinging and punching wildly. During the struggle while trying to restrain him, the gloved officer reached back for his walkie-talkie and clocked him full force with the butt end on his right temple. He dropped like a sack of rocks, out cold, twitching and trembling as the crowd of inmates watched through vengeful eyes. Instantly he was cuffed, bound wrists and ankles as the gloved officer radioed for assistance.

"Let's fuck these whiteboys up!" yelled one of the onlookers,

"Set it off!" yelled another, and a green wave of humanity consumed the two specks of gray, punching, kicking and stomping them as if they had stolen something from their mommas. It didn't take much to start a rebellion, especially by inmates who found themselves being used so often as objects of abuse and mistreatment such as they found themselves at Mohawk.

"Come on, we're on the *go-back*," I said to Alim and Musa, more so as a command than a suggestion.

"Wait man, everybody's leaving, let's move up," Alim said.

"Move up? We'd better move out!" said Musa, "We'd better get back to our dorms before they lock this place down with us in it."

Suddenly we found ourselves in the midst of a semi free-for-all. In the confusion, it seemed as if inmates who had long standing beefs, or gripes with each other took advantage of the chaos and went fisticuffs, right there on the spot. I noticed the remaining guards jumping over the serving counters which separated the kitchen from the mess hall. All the while a tape recording of a mechanical voice kept repeating the message, "Step back from the counters."

When the last guard hurdled the counter, the overhead spring-loaded gates came crashing down with an ear-deafening slam. We were surprised to find out that the officers had the kitchen as a safe haven or a built-in sanctuary for instances such as this. As we rushed out of the mess hall, running past the spot where the two guards were posted when we entered, we found they were not so lucky as to escape the mayhem, which incidentally was touched off by their cruel actions. Two guards were down and from the looks of their disfigured bodies, it would be a miracle if they were still alive.

"Move out the way, hurry up!" said Musa, to inmates who were forming a crowd a short distance from the mess hall.

I turned to look back and found that inmates who were at the front of the line and now were subsequently the last ones to exit, were intentionally trampling the two downed guards as they left. There was more than just a general dislike for these insensitive guards in gray who increasingly built a wall of animosity between the inmates and themselves. It was more like a burning hatred, and although I believe in looking first for the good in individuals, I found myself unsympathetic towards the two lifeless looking bodies that laid blood-soaked at the entrance to the mess hall.

"Man, let's get back to our dorms before the Crush gets here," said Musa.

"Do you think they'll really come? For this?" asked Alim.

"No telling what these crazy *kafirs* might do," said Musa.

Musa was referring to the notorious emergency response unit (ERU) called the *orange crush*, an elite group of extra-large men employed and trained by the state to implore SWAT-like tactics when necessary. Their sole job is to attain order in prisons that have been disrupted by inmates. Dressed in all orange, armed with batons and pepper spray, these men have been trained to hurt and intimidate and when they are summoned, their first objective is to leave no one standing, then dictate orders. They have been known to affect comments like, "The last thing I saw was orange."

By now, for the guards, help was on its way. I looked up the hill towards the administration building, which was approximately one hundred yards away, and saw guards filing out of the doorway and lining up alongside one another. I looked back at the mess hall and noticed through the windows that only four or five inmates remained inside. Behind them were approximately eight to ten officers wielding food trays, while pushing and shoving them, trying to force them outside. When the last inmate was out, one guard slammed the door behind him and locked it. As these inmates encountered the badly battered bodies of the first two guards, one of them weighing well over two hundred pounds, while running, stuttered his stride, then intentionally stomped on the head of the gloved officer and yelled, "How you like me now?!" as he joined the crowd laughing.

Looking at this scene made me shudder from the reality of knowing just how serious this situation had become. *That guard is dead for sure*, I thought. I noticed his body stiffen, suddenly tremble, then slowly relax after the inmate tried to crush his skull. *Some people are animals. Thank God they have jails in this society for people like that*, I thought. No one reprimanded this inmate. As a matter of fact, I recall hearing cheers and laughter and saw smiles on the faces of many as they stood around seemingly oblivious to, or just not caring about the consequences, which we were all about to suffer.

"Come on," I said, "Musa's right, let's get back to the dorms before we get trapped-off out here."

"*Assalamu alaikum*, I'll see you brothers later," said Musa nervously. He turned and wedged his shoulder between two inmates and yelled, "Comin' through," as he hurriedly pushed his way past and disappeared into the crowd.

"Brother Bilal," said Alim.

"Yeah brother," I said.

"We're in trouble, man," he said concernedly.

"Yeah, let's get outta here," I said, then paused and couldn't believe my eyes. "Check out the admin building on the hill," I said.

"Oh shit! Excuse my language, Bilal," said Alim.

He was as surprised as I to see in the distance, two guards coming through the doors of the administration building with leashed dogs from the K-9 squad. I had seen one dog before in the little less than a year since I had been at Mohawk. That was during a shake down when they suspected that drugs were being held by an inmate that was suspected of dealing. It was a large German shepherd, and I can remember standing next to my locker as the officer entered my cube. I was told, "Don't make a move," when the officer reached down to open my locker. I was watching the dog, which was looking in my eyes, and seemed to bare its teeth with every breath it took. I remember feeling absolutely powerless over this sobering duo, and conscientiously asking Allah to make this situation pass smoothly and let them quickly move on to the next inmate.

"The dogs! They got the dogs!" someone screamed, and the crowd of approximately three hundred inmates scattered like ants running toward their dorms.

Alim and I made a beeline to building twenty-two where he and I both locked, though in separate dorms. We approached the entrance with high expectations of shelter from the dogs and safety from the guards, but to our dismay the entrance doors were locked and we, along with approximately seventy other inmates who housed there also, found ourselves feeling stranded as though shipwrecked in a sea of wolves.

"They locked the fuckin' doors!" one inmate was screaming while he frantically yanked at the doors handles.

Turning around and looking back toward the administration building, you could see the guards still lining up as they now came running from the southeast and west ends of the compound. There inmates were still locked down and had not yet been released for *chow*. At any given time, there were sixty to seventy correction officers on duty to control a population of thirteen hundred inmates. As the guards entered the side entrances of the administration building in their standard gray, state issued uniforms, they exited through the front in full riot gear and fell in line, standing abreast until they numbered approximately fifty officers; they waited... In the minutes that passed, Alim and I had joined together with three other Muslims that locked with him in E dorm.

"What they waiting for?" said one nervous inmate who kept taking off his glasses and squinting as he kept a watchful eye on the activity surrounding the administration building.

"They gawn fuck us up," replied another.

As the crowd watched the activity of the guards, I glanced across to the west side of the compound at the seven smaller buildings facing us. They were housing for inmates also, and each one was a single dorm occupying fifty-five inmates. In front of each dorm were its residents, and they were in the same boat as we.

I noticed a group of *kufi*-clad Muslims beckoning to other Muslims and one, Brother Tarik (Ta-reek) calling out loud, "*Allahu Akbar* (God is the Greatest)," to get their attention.

"Brothers," I said, to get the attention of Alim and the others. I then pointed to the enlarging group of Muslims some sixty yards away. "Come on," I said, and without second thought or another word spoken, we parted from the crowd.

As the five of us walked toward the group, "Where's your *kufi*?" I asked Jabbar, one of the Muslims who locked in E dorm with Alim.

"I washed it when I got up, and left it to dry on my locker," he said.

"I keep tellin' you brothers to wear your *kufis*, at all

times," said Alim. "I don't know when y'all gawn learn," he said angrily.

"It's okay, I didn't mean to start a war," I said.

"It's not okay. You Brothers got to learn to wear your *kufis* all the time. If not for yourselves then at least in jail, so other brothers can identify and you can represent," he said.

Alim was right, now more than ever, it was very important to be able to distinguish between who was who, and if and when things got out of hand between inmates and officers, in the confusion you'd want to know where your friends are. The same went for when fighting broke out between members of gangs versus Muslims. When everyone's dressed in the same state greens, it's like playing basketball with both teams wearing the same uniforms while playing for the championship or playing-for-keeps...

As we approached the group, there was no time for socializing. Brother Hassan (Ha-saan), the *amir* (prince) or inside *imam* (spiritual adviser) was also one of the unfortunate to get caught out there.

"All those who don't have *kufis*, take off those tube socks they make us wear and tie one around each arm," he commanded as a drill sergeant to his troops. "All those with pens or pencils, come up front," he ordered again.

Then it hit me, we were preparing for war – Guerrilla fighting with pens and pencils against dogs and madmen armed with sticks and guns. This is crazy. *This is jail*, I thought to myself. I tuned out momentarily, the way one does when they're making *salaah* or like when one prays in public. *I don't want to be part of this*, I thought to myself. My eyes searched the surrounding area and as

51

I held my breath, it felt as if my heart was in my throat as it fluttered uncontrollably while I faced my fears. *What the hell am I doing here?* I thought. *This can't be for real*, I said to myself...

"*Allahu Akbar, Allahu Akbar*," I heard Brother Tarik, still calling other Muslims for assembly.

"All those with pens or pencils come up front," I heard once again.

As if my feet were an entity unto themselves, I found them taking me front and center reporting to Hassan. "Two," I said, "I got two pens, a black one and a red one."

In my mind, I was hopelessly enacting a scene, where I was handing him the pens, but it was for him to make a choice of colors, of which he would choose one to write with.

When he quickly snatched the closest one to him disregarding its color and asked, "Who ain't got a weapon?" I realized, if this was a dream, it would be a nightmare, but the glare of the morning sun and the cool breeze in my face assured me that I was wide awake.

"Brother Bilal, am I glad to see you," he said.

"*Assalamu alaikum*. Yeah right, misery loves company," I said anxiously. "You think we're lookin' at a beatdown?" I asked.

"You think we ain't?" Hassan replied.

I clenched my teeth, took a long stare at the guards, who I'm sure at this point were chomping at the bit and I took a deep breath. I reached down and tightened my boot laces, preparing myself for action. I thought whether or not I would be better off if I had worn my sneakers. *No*, I concluded, *boots are better for keeping the dogs at bay. The dogs*, I thought. *Oh my God, dogs too, how do you fight a dog?* I wondered.

"What are they doing? They got more dogs," someone said, and three more officers stepped through the doors of the administration building with leashed K-9s.

As they stood in front of the fifty or so officers, there now numbered five K-9s alongside their handlers, barking like hounds ready for the hunt. They still waited.

"Brother Bilal, call the *Adhan*," ordered Hassan.

Now? I asked.

Not now, right now, he said.

I regularly took on this responsibility at *Jummah* on Fridays and at prayer times when multiple Muslims were together and I was present.

I dropped to the ground and started making a dry ablution called *Tayammum*. It is to symbolically use dust as water, to wash before praying. I didn't bother to ask why we were going to have a congregational prayer at this time. Once I thought about it, I decided it only made sense that if one had the opportunity to die in a state of grace, they would do so. And prayer for a Muslim is the cleansing of his sins. I rose to my feet, I tuned out, I got my bearings. *The sun, the sun rises in the east*, I said to myself. And I faced the morning sun, till its rays warmed my face through the soft cool breeze. I squinted and felt as if its blinding light shone for me and me alone.

I raised my head higher and looked to the heavens, "I'm ready to die, if this be Your will," I said softly. Standing front and center I then raised my hands to my head, plugged my ears with my fingers, and to the top of my lungs, with "*Allahu Akbar, Allahu Akbar*," I started the

Adhan, the call to prayer. When I finished, I lowered my arms, and heard in a lower voice the *Iqamah*, being called by Tarik, signaling the start of congregational prayer.

Brother Hassan came along side me and with the smile of a man of dignity, looked me in the eyes and just said softly, "My brother."

I smiled back and said, "Let's do this."

I then, took a step back joining the front rank behind Hassan as he led us in prayer. When we finished making *salat*, everyone was on their feet in an instant. My eyes scanned the scene again and noticed, the line of officers now numbered about seventy and they were still coming through the doors.

"They got more guards," someone yelled.

"They're callin' 'em in from the outside," said another.

"Brother Hassan, what we gawn do man?" asked someone else.

"We gawn chill," said Hassan. "Don't nobody panic. Look, we got trapped off, but it ain't no thing, we gawn deal with this like men. We gawn deal with this like Muslims," he said.

"*Allahu Akbar* (God is the greatest)!" and "*Alhamdulillah* (thank God)!" was shouted by a few.

"Whatever happens to us, you gotta' remember, we put ourselves here and ain't nobody else's fault but our own. Yeah, they got dogs, but we got Allah and each other, and any man who thinks he won't be able to use that pen or pencil, pass it off to someone who does," Hassan paused. "Listen," he started again, "We ain't out to commit murder or trying to hurt nobody, we ain't livin' like that. But if you are assaulted for no reason, in the eyes of Allah you have a right to defend yourself. Now if you choose not to, that's on you, but you do have that option," he said. "I want two ranks: pens and pencils up front," he commanded. "Keep 'em outta' sight, put 'em in your back pocket. You guys with the socks on your arms, put a double knot in 'em. If we get a chance, we gonna let 'em know you're Muslims."

"Brother Hassan, why we got to suffer for something some fool *kafirs* did? Didn't no Muslims do nonna dat," said a young Muslim not yet in his twenties.

"You wearing green my brother, somebody in green did it. Right now they don't care who did what, They just lookin' for blood. You see that boy slam the door shut on two of his own, and left 'em out here for dead? They think even less of you, get used to it," he said. "What's your name, young brother?" asked Hassan, of the young Muslim who evidently was a new arrival, even I had never seen him before.

"Jihad," he said, "Abdullah Jihad."

"Oh, you like to fight I bet," said Hassan and from the young Muslim's face, he managed to eke out an affirmative smile. "Well let's hope you don't get a chance to prove it today. Not only does *jihad* mean war, but it also means to struggle within yourself, to do the right thing. A young brother like you should be in school tryin' to better yourself," Hassan paused. Jihad was in the front rank with a pen still clutched in his right fist. "No offense, my young brother. Keep your pen, but we need our youth to perpetuate the truth."

Then Hassan put his arm across young Jihad's shoulders and placed him in the middle of the second rank as to keep him out of harm's way as best he could. The two ranks of Muslims assembled now totaled twenty-six and were still no match to do battle with an opposing force that outnumbered them three to one and still climbing.

"Where they getting those dogs from?" someone cried out.

I looked up to see. Now a total of ten K-9s at the forefront of a wall of guards, that by now had almost doubled since before we started prayer. Evidently, they were coming in by the busloads from neighboring jails in the same hub. There were three other prisons within a six-mile radius of Mohawk, and extra help could be quickly summoned, even on a volunteer basis if it meant cracking a few sculls for recreation.

"It was too good to be true," said a voice of disappointment directly behind me.

I turned my head to see Musa, who had left Alim and me ten minutes earlier outside the mess hall. He looked to be in a state of shock at the thought of his dream of packing up and going home to be shattered by a freak of circumstance so close to his release date.

"I'ma die in here. I always knew I'd never make it back home alive," he said remorsefully.

Musa's jaws were tightened to a vice-like clench, as he stared at the guards up the hill. There were no words of consolation to be spoken, as for me, the feeling was mutual.

"OK, they rollin' on us," shouted Hassan, and I looked to see the impressive show of force begin their march down the well-manicured grass hill toward us, the inmates in the north sector of the compound.

"Brother Hassan!" I called, "What's the plan?" I asked.

"No plan!" he continued loudly, "Let's just play it by ear. It's already written in the books. What's gawn happen's gawn happen. Besides, if Allah wanted none of us to be here, He'da found another group of sorry souls to do this bid."

Muslims believe in destiny and Hassan had just reminded everyone of just that.

Now my anxiety peaked. The thought of surviving a beatdown terrified me, more so than the actual infliction of it. *I'm a fighter,* I said to myself. *I can handle whatever comes my way. A guard is just a man in a uniform with a big stick and maybe a gun. I'll just take it as it comes and do as much damage as I can along the way. Besides, the worst pain will come after whatever happens anyway, during the healing process, so don't worry I'll survive it,* I told myself. I had no way to process my dilemma with logic, so I was grasping for straws trying to make sense of it all. Then reality set in again and I paused, and thought, *the dogs, the dogs, the dogs…*

My heart sank as I stared at the guards' front line. Watching the dogs barking and yelping, some of them on their hind legs pulling and jerking their handlers, seemed to drain me of my energy and courage each time I'd psych myself up. I found myself continually rethinking my plan of action…*Why are the Muslims the first line of defense?* I thought selfishly and I glanced toward building number twenty-two only to discover a group of approximately twenty-five inmates hurriedly making their way toward us.

"Brother Hassan!" I called.

Hassan was standing like a statue made of steel, with his hands clasped across his groin, expressionless as he stared at what could be the death of us all. He turned his head with a quick snap as did the others who were silently watching the guards.

"Netas" I said, while motioning with my head towards the direction of the approaching group. They were being led by my dormmate Rico. Rico was the Netas' gang leader, tough-as-nails, and it seemed only fitting that a man of his character would be the first to step into hellfire if need be.

Hassan smiled, "The more the merrier," he said.

I looked across to the four buildings on my right, and inmates started to trickle by ones and twos, then threes and small groups of inmates now started making their way toward us. Then, as if nobody wanted to be the last one, they came running from all directions until not an inmate could be seen at any of the building's entrances. They all fell in line abreast on both sides of us. As they were scrambling into position. It felt as if a heavy weight was lifted from my chest. I distinctly remember the feeling of being able to breathe freely again. I thought of what it must be like for schooling fish being chased by predators. *Someone's going to get eaten. I just hope it's not me.*

Then, with an alarming and ear deafening blast, the sirens went off with an intermittent, *blatt, blatt, blatt,* from one set and, *ahhgooahh, ahhgooahh,* from another.

"They ain't comin' to talk," yelled Hassan over his shoulder.

Seconds earlier, you could hear the dogs coming closer, but now we had to rely strictly on our sight…With my sense of hearing impaired by the sirens, I focused more intently on the wall of guards. I watched how it swayed its way down the hill coming at us like a pregnant desert sidewinder snake, with the K-9s being its unborn brood at its belly.

Snakes lay eggs, I chuckled in my mind. Then thought, *how could I laugh at a time like this? Come on, get it together*, I told myself. *My pen*, I thought. Then I reached in my back pocket, took the pen's cover and as hard as I could I twisted it onto the back, exposing the tip. I maneuvered it around my palm until it felt comfortable. Then as if the snake gave birth to its brood, its belly burst into its litter as the dogs came at us like greyhounds chasing a track rabbit. Like large bands of spring steel, leaping forth and snapping shut in perpetual motion, the dogs went on the attack. I noticed up and down the endless line of inmates many of them making the sign of the cross, a few of them kissing their crucifixes, and one Asian inmate holding something in his mouth that was attached to a lace of leather around his neck. These men were well aware that the possibility of death hung deceptively heavy in the air, even on a day such as glorious as this.

I watched the lead dog, a large black German shepherd with dark rust-colored markings, lunge at the line of inmates about fifty feet to my left. Inmates scattered to the right and to the left of this snarling, snapping fur ball of vicious K-9 ferocity. Except one unfortunate inmate who became securely attached by the throat to the business end of this trained man-eater. As the dog stood over him, pinning him down, his paws danced back and forth across this inmate's body. While the inmate wriggled and squirmed, gasping desperately for one last breath of life, the dog shook him violently with relentless persistence; until with no more resistance its teeth broke free from the man's neck suddenly and it wheeled and turned with a mouth full of entrails. After shaking the life out of what seemed to be the man's esophagus and its innards, it suddenly stopped, dropped the remains and charged another unfortunate inmate, causing him to fall prey by the same inhumane method of execution to this seemingly crazed beast. I remained still, frozen with fear and felt the muscles in my neck taut as tent lines as I watched in horror. *My God!* I thought *They're going to kill us.*

The dogs penetrated our line at various points and wreaked havoc and maimed at every point of attack. Inmates ran for their lives as the guards watched this melodrama unfold, being scored to the tune of the sirens. Suddenly as if I was blindsided by an NFL line-backer, or more like being slapped with a hundred-pound sack of potatoes, I was hit from behind by my worst nightmare. I felt a crunch, then the pressure of what seemed like my left bicep being crushed in a hydraulic press. I found myself being knocked off my feet and falling toward the ground, firmly gripped in jaws, laden with the smell of death.

"Grrrrr," it growled.

My whole upper torso rumbled from the vibration of this growling beast. As we looked in each other's eyes, I somehow managed to show this animal more rage than fear.

"You crazy???" I screamed in the animals face only inches away.

Now I felt as if I was on autopilot. *Survival of the fittest* came to mind. I was healthy and strong, and self-preservation had somehow instinctively carried me through victoriously by the moves I made next. I had owned a few large dogs in my time, but none had ever turned on me. Yet I knew by applying pressure with my thumb and middle finger to the rear of the animal's jaws, he would relax his grip, or at least I hoped and probably even prayed it would. It worked. As we hit the ground the animal still had a firm grip on my arm. I was flat on my back and with one tremendous tug, it jerked me up into sitting position. I still had my pen firmly gripped in my right hand, so I swung my arm hard and buried the pen in the animal's upper chest. The dog yelped and released me, only to suddenly turn and viciously bite my right hand, puncturing it completely through with its fangs.

"Arghhhh!" I yelled from the pain.

As this animal held my hand in its mouth growling and shaking it violently, I simultaneously roared back at it loudly, and slapped the animal as hard as I could with the heel of my left hand, behind its ear. It released me again, reared back, and lunged at my face. Looking into the mouth of this large, black, Doberman pinscher, I could see the rippled rows of flesh on the roof of its mouth between its frighteningly large white teeth. For some reason, I felt I was winning this fight between man and beast and was sure of it when I threw my hands in front of my face as it grabbed me again; this time by my left forearm, leaving its snout vulnerable, and wide open to a hammer blow delivered by my right fist. The dog yelped loudly released me again and snorted violently as if it were sneezing. It sneezed repeatedly and gave me enough time to get to my feet. In a way I felt sorry for this exquisitely beautiful jet-black animal as it stood there trying to regain control of its faculties. It sneezed one last time then started licking at the pen, or what was left of it, protruding from its left side. I noticed a small stream of blood forming a puddle under the animal's left paw as it held it raised, favoring it, while licking its wound.

I felt now was my chance to retreat. I took one step back and then as if this pathetic-looking animal was given a new lease on life, it stared at me boldly and I realized then that it was not about to let me leave alive if it could help it. It suddenly stood alert, disregarding its pain. Then with its ears erect, it looked me directly in the eyes with a long cold stare. It suddenly laid its ears back and charged me with lightning speed. I was knocked to the ground again, straight back, this time wrapping my thighs around the dog in a scissor lock as it grabbed me by the throat. I was terrified but I was also a bit more than just determined not to die by the jaws of a dog. I was pinned down. Next, as if by a miracle, the dog paused and violently coughed while still holding me by the throat. I felt a gush of warmed liquid across my neck and shoulders; it was the dog's blood that had hemorrhaged into its lungs by the pen wound. I grabbed the animal's snout, feeling for its jaws. My thumb and middle finger found its back teeth and as hard as I could, I squeezed. Its mouth opened wide, and I was free. I was enraged to say the least and now I felt I wanted to put an end to the life of this dog once and for all. As I held the dog with my right palm over its snout, I grabbed its lower jaw with my left palm over its tongue, then leaned on my right side, rolling the dog on its side. The dog yelped as the pen disappeared into the animal's body. As I braced my right arm firmly on the ground with the weight of my body, I then gathered all the strength I could muster and with one hard thrust, I spread its jaw until it snapped hyperextended. The dog broke free the instant I relaxed the scissor hold I had around it. It then limped slowly away on three legs with its lower jaw dangling loosely before it laid down and curled its mortally wounded body some five yards away.

This dog was not going to attack again, and what it did next almost brought tears to my eyes. Realizing this dog was only one of ten of these man-bred killing machines, I feared the worst was not over. I also knew that this animal was in possession of what I felt was the only thing that stood between me and my demise, my pen. It had clearly been the equalizing factor in my victorious outcome this time, and hopefully there'd not be a next. Fear of being attacked unexpectedly again by another, I quickly got to my feet and cautiously approached the downed dog. It laid there curled and crying like a homesick puppy, looking up at me with sympathetic eyes.

"Nice doggie," I said, while reaching apprehensively for what little was left exposed of the pen's cover, protruding from its side. To my surprise, the dog started briskly wagging its stub of a tail as if it were glad to see me. Now defenseless and dying, it seemed to want to be man's best friend, and as I looked in its eyes, it looked as if it wanted to be comforted. "Dammit dog," I cursed it for making me responsible for its inevitable death. I gripped the pen's cover with the tips of my thumb and index finger, all the while checking the dog's eyes for a change in its attitude. When I realized it was incapable of doing me anymore harm, I quickly yanked the pen from its ribcage and checked my surroundings.

It was hard to believe that men killing men for the sake of entertainment was sanctioned by the state. This was a camp, not a maximum facility. Everyone here was scheduled to go home within the next five years. These were men who were coming down off long jail sentences, or not doing more than five-year bids. Jail has a way of bringing the best and the worst out of men, inmates and guards alike, but with each given day, one can never be sure of which. Even the guards, after twenty years of service, would have completed eight years behind bars themselves. A big difference between them though, besides going home every night, is that the guards can do virtually anything they want and get away with it.

Inmates were scattered everywhere in the north sector. Our line was broken badly, but not completely abandoned. Every time a dog would chase an inmate and subdue him, inmates would converge on the animal kicking, then pulling at their legs and tails. The Muslims literally had their hands full in the form of a huge German shepherd. I saw one dog dead and mangled about forty feet away. Its twisted body laid underfoot a group of Muslims who had another K-9 outstretched by all fours. As the four men, one at each leg, seemed to be playing a game of tug-of-war with the animal, it somehow managed to still snarl and snap its teeth from side to side at the two men holding its front paws. Then one of the men leaned back with a hind leg firmly in his grasp, and started yanking it, till it suddenly tore free from the dogs' hind quarters as he stumbled backwards and fell to the ground. *Three down, seven to go*, I thought.

Then, as if someone pulled the plug, the sirens stopped. I heard the barking of two dogs, and assumed they were alive and well. I heard the yelping of one dog and turned to see the dog with its rear leg removed, propping itself up with its front legs while it dragged itself aimlessly, yelping from the pain. I heard men yelling to each other, some screaming in pain from their wounds suffered by the dogs, some crying in anguish at the loss of their friends, some just being boisterous and loud caught up in the excitement of the moment. It was these boisterous type men, who in the face of death, I've seen become martyrs and heroes. It sounded like the aftermath of one of a few fire fights I survived along the Me Kong River in Cambodia, SE Asia. Back in the war... I envisioned one of these boisterous men going off the deep end and charging the line of guards, like corporal "Crazy Barry" Gates.

Despondent from the loss of over half of our squad, without warning he yelled, "I'm tired of all this shit, Goddammit!" jumped to his feet and charged the well-hidden North Vietnamese soldiers yelling, "I'll see you motha fuckas in Hell!"

With his M-16 rifle set on full auto, he ran blazing the foliage in front of him 'till his magazine was empty. He never stopped running while he ejected the empty magazine, flipped it over and reloaded his weapon with a full one that was taped alongside and upside down to the empty for a speedy reload. As he worked the slide to reload his weapon, three Vietcong guerrillas jumped from the high grass. Barry cut down two of them before he went down in a hail of bullets fired by the third, discharging the balance of his magazine into the ground as his hand held a death grip on the rifle's trigger. I had run out of .223 caliber M-16 rifle ammunition and had my model 1911, .45 caliber automatic pistol in hand with two rounds left. I habitually always counted discharged rounds from my handgun. A well-placed shot eliminated the threat of the third guerrilla, and I was left with one round until we took a body count, and I replenished my supply of ammo from my dead comrades.

These prison guards are going to waste us, I thought. I was still in combat mode from fighting the dog; it sounded like a battle zone to me, men crying out in anguish. Instinctively I hit the dirt and covered up, anticipating the sounds of the comparatively slow report of .50 caliber machine gun fire with rockets and bullets flying overhead. It was the closest I've come to being shell shocked in all the years since the war. I had never acknowledged showing symptoms of PTSD (Post Traumatic Stress Disorder), or ever suffering flashbacks, but I guess it took prison to make me question whether or not I had been a victim of this condition like thousands of cases that go untreated throughout the U.S.

As I lay motionless, I started to sense the pain of my wounds and smell the strong scent of dog on my clothing. *The dogs*, I thought. This time I slowly got to my feet. The more I thought of the pain the more I felt the throbbing in my right hand. My left shirtsleeve was ripped as was the sleeve of my thermal shirt underneath. My whole left arm was starting to swell and stiffen, and blood was dripping from my left hand. I couldn't see any of the other dogs, but

I still heard their barking and from the sound of it, they were just barking and not attacking anyone. I looked at the dog that attacked me and saw a few inmates standing over it, looking down and watching its body convulse as it now lay flat on its side regurgitating blood. I turned to look at the wall of guards and I felt pain on both sides of my neck. The skin around my back and waist were getting tight from the drying blood coughed up by the dog when he held me by the throat. I looked a mess and felt even worst. The guards hadn't made a move. They kept a safe distance away from us and the dogs through the whole ordeal. Now I heard the dog handler's whistles and the barking abruptly stopped. I saw two German shepherds running up the hill then fall in line alongside their handlers. We got eight, I said to myself, and for a brief moment I found myself grinning, overwhelmed by the feeling of victory at their loss of all but two dogs.

"Bilal, you alright!" said Alim, excitedly, as he looked me squarely in the eyes while gripping me firmly by both shoulders.

"I was, before you got here," I said jokingly. "My arm," I warned him, and he relaxed his grip.

"What happened?" he asked.

"I'll write a book about it later," I said while grimacing from the pain. "Everybody ok?" I asked.

"Nah man," he said, "Brother Hassan got it bad, a couple of other brothers got tore up. Come on, I'll help you," he said, and he put an arm around my waist and lead me toward the group of Muslims about fifty feet away.

Upon approach, Hassan was being helped to the ground where he sat holding his left cheek with his *kufi*.

Blood covered the whole front of his shirt and down his left leg past his knee.

"Hassan," I said to Alim, and I steered us toward him. "You don't look too good, can you talk?" I asked.

Hassan looked at me and shook his head, *no*. He was losing blood fast and needed immediate attention. I knelt down next to him to take a closer look at his wound and he moved his head away implying, *don't touch it.*

"Stay still, I'm not gonna touch it," I said, "I just wanna get a look at you."

As I inspected Hassan's face, I could see he was holding his cheek in place, with his *kufi* being used as a compress. His cheek was torn from the corner of his mouth like a flap, and you could see his teeth through the gaping hole each time he repositioned the *kufi*. There was a puncture wound high on his neck that flowed slowly but constantly pulsated.

"I think it got your jugular vein, I'm just gonna press on it," I said.

Hassan nodded, *yes*.

My right hand was swollen pretty badly, and I pointed to the wound with my pinky finger. "Alim," I said.

"Yeah, I see it," he said.

"Press about an inch below it," I said, and with pressure from Alim's thumb, the flowing stopped instantly.

"You guys are in bad shape," said Alim. "Brother Musa!" he yelled. Musa was about twenty feet away inspecting a bite wound that he had suffered on his right calf.

"Yo-yo!" he answered and quickly limped over to us. "Y'all brothers OK? Y'all don't look OK," he said concernedly as Hassan leaned over and drooled blood onto the grass.

"Musa, hold your thumb here," said Alim, and they quickly switched places.

"We gotta' get them to the infirmary," he said as he stood up and looked around. "*Allahu Akbar!*" he shouted. "Everybody, gather round," he said, and the Muslims reassembled.

I sat next to Hassan while Musa knelt behind him keeping pressure on his neck wound. "What's them holes in your neck, Bilal?" said Musa.

"Damn dog," I said, and I motioned with my head to the dog I killed some fifty feet away.

"Y'all brothers could'a got killed, this is a damn disgrace," he said. The anger was mounting inside him. "What they gawn do next, shoot us down like dogs?" he yelled loudly at the guards up the hill, only some two hundred feet away.

"Don't give 'em any ideas, they may take you up on it," I said.

"Anybody else hurt?" asked Alim of the now gathered Muslims.

After taking a headcount there were seven of us who were bitten, of which Hassan and I were the worst. As I sat in the grass alongside Hassan, reality started to sink in. Hassan was in really bad shape. I wasn't too well off myself. These three hundred inmates were responsible for possibly the death of at least two guards. They were also responsible for the probable death of eight K-9s, which were the property of the state. This was a riot situation and both sides had the casualties to prove it. I saw two inmates killed by a dog. I'm sure there were more, and whatever the damage totaled, these inmates would be held accountable. There'd be long obituaries for the dead and short investigations for the living and only God knows how much more time we'd all get tacked on to our bids for this uprising, if any.

Suddenly, "This is the warden," came over the loudspeakers. "Stop your rioting now!" the voice demanded. It was being transmitted from the administration building.

"Rioting? Who in the hell is rioting? Oh, these motha fuckas is crazy!"

"Fuck you square badge motha fuckas!"

These were just some of the things I heard coming from the inmates as I sat keeping a close eye on Hassan. I hadn't yet inspected my own wounds and now I took the time to do so. Musa was on his knees and had one hand on Hassan's neck, keeping pressure on his jugular vein, and with the other, he was inspecting the bite wound on his leg.

"Jabbar," I said. He was standing next to me looking at the guards as was everyone else. "Give me a hand here, brother," and as I held my left arm up, "The button," I said.

He bent down and after he undone the button, he pulled my shirtsleeve up exposing the white sleeve of my thermal which was now blood red. As he peeled back the thermal by the sleeve band, "I hope you test negative" he said.

"No diggidy," I replied.

He was referring to the results of the HIV test that was given to every inmate when they become a ward of the state and I was colloquially responding in so many words, you bet, or in a word, yes.

"You bleedin' bad, Bilal," he said.

Then he untied a sock from one of his arms and used it as a tourniquet to slow the bleeding of my left arm. While he tied a knot in the tourniquet, his bare head reminded me of the scolding Alim had given him earlier regarding his *kufi*. I managed to take my *kufi* off with my bitten right hand and precariously place it on Jabbar's head.

"Even trade," I said, "Wear it in good health. I have three more, don't worry about It."

We exchanged smiles.

"Thanks Bilal, I will," he said as he adjusted it properly and looked at me for approval. I gave him a nod of affirmation. He then removed the sock from his other arm, rose to his feet proudly and stared at the guards.

"You will form a single line and put your ID cards in one neat pile in the center of the walkway when you're told to do so," said the warden over the speakers. "You will then return to your dorms quietly and await further instructions. All those in need of medical attention will remain behind. The sooner you do this, the sooner the injured will be seen."

Inmates started to gather on the walkway coming from all directions, some with ID cards in hand hoping to expedite their return to the shelter of their dorms.

"Hold your ground!" demanded Alim of the Muslims. "These *kafirs* spilled Muslim blood, and we ain't havin' it," he said.

"We can't fight 'em all," Tarik said, sensibly. "It would be suicide," he added.

Alim thought for a moment, then sighed deeply while nodding his head. "You right," he paused. "You right," he repeated. "They gawn pay for this one day. Brother Bilal!" he turned and called. "Y'all brothers gawn be alright?" he asked, referring to the injured.

"You know it," I said, "Don't worry, y'all brothers break out so we can get served."

He walked up to Hassan, Musa and I and knelt on one knee in front of Hassan who had his eyes closed fighting the pain in his jaw. He stared at Hassan's wounds, then looked at me and shook his head in disgust from the whole incident. Then he simultaneously embraced the three of us, taking care not to touch the left side of Hassan's face.

"*Assalamu alaikum*," he said as he stood up and turned toward the guards.

"*Walaikum salaam*," we responded.

As he stood panning the line of guards from left to right, I watched the back of his head slowly pivot then suddenly stop. "Hey Miller!" he shouted at the guards. I knew Officer Miller was his detail supervisor in the metal shop where Alim worked as an instructor. "Take care of my boys, man," he shouted while pointing directly at him. "Take care of my boys," he repeated in a threatening tone. Alim turned around. "Let's bounce," he said "Y'all brothers ready to go?" he asked of the other Muslims. "All y'all wit bites, chill, no tellin' what them damn dogs got," he said in disgust. We were left with well wishes from the group as they passed us by and walked toward the gathering crowd on the walkway.

A group of thirty or so guards including the two K-9s with their handlers were approaching the inmates that had gathered. As they came to a stop, "Drop 'em here!" shouted a sergeant while pointing his finger at the ground in front of him. "Your cards, gimme your damn cards and hurry up," he yelled.

I watched the inmates, one by one, drop their cards and return to their respective dorms. During the departure of the inmates, a state van pulled up to the mess hall, and the driver, along with the help of other officers, recovered their two downed co-workers. It was impossible for me to tell at that time whether or not these guards were dead, but from the looks of their limp bodies as they placed them in the van, one could only imagine the worst and hope for the best, both for their sakes and ours. All was fairly quiet, except for an occasional painful moan from injured inmates in the distance.

"Hey Bilal," said Musa, quietly.

He was still kneeling behind Hassan and me, keeping pressure on Hassan's neck wound with his thumb.

"He's shivering like crazy, and I can barely feel his pulse anymore," he said.

"You know everyone has a pulse in their thumb," I said.

"Yeah, I know," he said, "but I tried it with my fingers too."

Hassan was sitting in the lotus position, and had his left elbow on his knee, supporting the weight of his head with his palm. The *kufi* in his hand was blood soaked, and blood ran down his arm, onto his thigh, then into the grass, forming a puddle in which he sat trembling.

"Hassan," I said. He didn't respond. "Hassan!" I repeated loudly. There was absolutely no response, and watching him tremble with the shivers, I knew he was in trouble. "Shock, he's going into shock!" I said, and we all gathered around him. "Cover him up, we gotta keep him warm," I said, and in an instant Hassan had two state jackets draped over him, front and back.

"Easy come, easy go," I heard Jabbar say, as I watched him remove the *kufi* I had just given to him, then gingerly place it on Hassan's head and adjust it with his fingertips.

He did it with a combination of caution trying not to disturb him while in pain and with reverence, which we all had for our *amir*, Hassan. There were still around forty or fifty inmates still left on line waiting to drop their cards, while injured inmates dotted the sprawling grounds everywhere in need of medical attention some in more serious condition than others.

"Man, they gotta hurry up," said Musa while peering at the smaller group of guards at the front of the line of inmates. "We gawn bleed to death out here if they don't hurry up and take care of us," he added.

"Oh, they'd just love that!" said one of the Muslims. "Sittin' around the dinner table, bragging to their kids about how many niggas they killed on the job today," he said.

"We gotta get these brothers to the infirmary quick," said Musa, referring to Hassan and myself. "Ay, yo, officers!" he yelled at the smaller group of guards who were collecting ID cards. He got their attention, but it went ignored. "Officeeer!" he yelled again, and the second attempt produced the same results until we all joined in calling them loudly in rowdy fashion and in angry tones.

Three officers parted from their group and came to our

assistance. I noticed one of the guards was Officer Miller, who Alim had instructed to take care of us. All threats in jail are not to be taken lightly, and obviously Miller was taking no chances. They stopped at a safe distance from us because of our earlier rowdiness and now our angry and defiant postures, "OK kneel down, I want all-a-yous on your knees," ordered one of the guards.

"Man, you mus be crazy," said Musa.

"We're Muslins, we bow to no man," said another.

"We all bit up, what we got ta kneel for?" said someone behind me.

"Aye, look!" I interrupted. "All we want to do is to get this man to the hospital," I directed to the guards as I gestured to Hassan sitting next to me.

"What's under his coat?" asked one of the officers.

"He's under his damn coat, he's bleedin' to death" snapped Musa. "Allah forgive me," he uttered under his breath for losing control of his emotions. He then snatched the front state jacket from Hassan's shoulder and exposed the gruesome sight of his blood loss to the officers.

"Aw, man, cover him back up," said Miller as he screwed his face in disbelief.

Musa then quickly replaced the jacket around Hassan's shoulders, looked at Miller and calmly said, "He's in shock and he's dying, and he's got to get some help, now. Will you help him, please?"

"A-ra-uhm, let me find out what the sarge is gonna do here," Miller said indecisively. "Come on" he said to the other two guards, then turned and left.

As the guards walked away it was obvious that there was no sense of urgency in their pace.

"Prejudice bastards!" said Musa, "They gawn let us die out here" he said. "I can't wait till I get outta' here next month, I'ma kill the first white motha fucka I see," he said angrily.

"Come on brother," I said calmly. "That would make you one of them," I said, referring to their *kafir* status. Minutes passed and we watched the last inmate drop his card and leave. The sergeant signaled to the wall of over one hundred guards still waiting in reserve, then they slowly headed towards the administration building, withdrawing leisurely like a crowd leaving a concert. The remaining guards numbered about forty, all totaled, and it was their job to do the pending dirty work of transporting the dead and injured, to either the facility's infirmary or an outside hospital, depending upon the seriousness of the injury.

Miller returned alone…

"I need yous cards," he said.

"What about our brother here?" asked Musa. "You gotta get him outta here," he said.

"We got some guys a lot worse off than him," said Miller.

"Worse?" snapped Musa. "How can you get any worse than him?" he said angrily. "He's dying dammit!" he shouted. "He's dying, and y'all playin' games with people's lives. We'll carry him ourselves, I'll fuckin' carry him myself, alone," he added.

"Uh, look fellas," said Miller, "I'm just doin' my job. I just gotta have your cards first," he said.

"Then will you get him to the hospital?" asked Musa.

"We'll see," answered Miller, and he held out his hand for the cards.

"We need a guarantee," said Musa.

"I can't do yous that," said Miller, "but we'll see," he said again.

From the corner of my eye, as I sat watching the nervous re-posturing of Miller's stance, I saw Musa turn his head and heard him whisper the word hostage to the group. Miller still had his hand out waiting for the ID cards.

"Yeah," I heard Jabbar signal back to Musa softly.

"Uh huh," someone else uttered and Musa stood up from behind Hassan to prepare his attack on Miller.

The moment he released the hold on Hassan's neck, Hassan fell backwards, his left shoulder hitting Musa's right leg, causing Hassan to hit the ground shoulder first. Hassan was lying flat out, with his eyes open, in a blank stare. Everyone looked shocked. Musa knelt beside him, opened Hassan's shirt, and pressed his ear against Hassan's chest. Moments later…

"He's dead," said Musa, as he rose to his feet and stared at Miller, jaws pulsating while clenching his teeth.

"Hey Sarge," said Miller, into his walkie-talkie while backing up to a safe distance away. "We got another one expired over here, the Muslims," he said, then he turned and quickly walked back, joining his co-workers without collecting our ID cards.

CHAPTER 3

Infirmary

The nightmare was finally over when I reached the infirmary. Before being treated, I was made to lay on a gurney naked, where, because of my injuries, I was washed down by an inmate medical assistant named Oliver.

"What happened over there on the north side this morning?" he asked.

"Man, you wouldn't believe me if I told you," I said in a somber tone. I was still in somewhat a state of shock from this morning's turn of events.

"Try me," he said. "I can believe those twelve bodies in the morgue I gotta wash down after the medical examiner looks at 'em," he said.

"Twelve?" I said. "Twelve bodies?" I repeated.

"Yeah, one of 'ems a Muslim," he said. "I hope they didn't stir up no shit in this jail," he said. "My father is a Muslim; I know how them motha fuckas think. If you spill Muslim blood, they'll cut your fucking head off. They believe Muslim blood is sacred," he said while putting on a pair of surgical gloves, preparing to wash the dry blood from my back and waist.

"Your father's a Muslim?" I asked.

"Yeah, a real goodie-goodie, too fuckin passive though," he said.

"Whata you mean?" I asked.

"Well," he started, "like I never heard him raise his voice in anger, and he always seemed to have an answer for everything. Funny thing though, he always seemed to be right," he added.

"You're not a Muslim, I gather." I said.

"Nah man, him and my mother split up when I was a little tyke. She's Jewish and they were always arguing about going back to Israel or staying here in the U.S." he said.

"Oh, so your Jewish?" I said.

"Hell no!" he said, "I sure as hell ain't gonna put a label on the God I believe in. If I did, it would probably be Smith and Wesson or Colt, or some other big gun manufacture's name. Now there's a God everybody listens to."

"You may be right about that," I said.

"Yeah, the power," he said. "Fuuuck, after a couple a six-packs, I've seen God have 'em bowin' and on their stomachs in the isles at 7-11," he said and laughed.

Oliver spoke like a true lost soul. Problem was, he should have listened more to his parents, but he was so busy listening to his God, that he never heard the Devil talking to him. Well Oliver eventually learned that I was a Muslim and he assured me that he would take special care when it came to Hassan – that he would make sure his *kufi* travelled with him in the body bag when they sent his remains back home.

Three weeks had gone by, and I was still hospitalized. My wounds were almost healed. They repaired a severed vein in my left arm, and I could open and close my right hand to a loose fist. It was the second week of June and temperatures went well into the eighties on some afternoons. Sometimes, I'd hear in the distance, the sound of the tractors and mower's engines of the lawns and grounds crew working outside the gate on the perimeter of the jail. I'd watch through the window for hours sometimes, critiquing their every move. "He should have cut that area counter-clockwise," I would say. "Who is that driving the Ford tractor? Don't they know they have to raise the blades in that spot?" were some of the things I found myself saying out loud, in the privacy of my hospital room.

It was a nice break from the daily routine of prison life. I hadn't heard, "On the *go back*! or *"On the chow!"* or *"On the rec!"* or *"On the count!"* or on the this or that being yelled by the guards for a few weeks now and I wasn't missing it. One thing I did miss though was *Jummah*. *Jummah* was held at Muslim services every Friday at one o'clock. It was a time to get together with all the Muslims in the jail. We'd wrestle, tell jokes, quiz each other on religious facts, and congregate like one big happy family. At the end, we'd all pray together side by side in tight rows, shoulder to shoulder in perfectly straight ranks, standing and prostrating like good servants of Allah. Ahhh, I said to myself, as I twisted the back of my head from side to side, nestling it snugly deeper into the pillow of my adjustable contour, hospital bed. Hassan came to mind, *Jummah won't be the same without him*, I thought. Jabbar and the others will be glad to hear that he wore his *kufi* back home.

Nearing the last week of June, one month had passed, and boredom seemed to get more and more constant the more I gained mobility of my arm and hand. Early one morning after showering and making morning prayer, I laid back down and dozed off as usual of my new routine. Inmates in the infirmary were not responsible for regular program movement and the confining quarters of the infirmary left much to be desired in the form of exercise and freedom to move about. I welcomed a rude awakening on this morning by an infirmary staff nurse named Ms. Tucker.

"Zero-two-one-two! Zero-two-one-two!" she repeated.

Zero-two-one-two were the last four numbers of my inmate ID number and it's how the medical staff referred to each patient.

"Pack up!" she said loudly.

I didn't actually see her, only a bold strip of light on the wall opposite my bed slowly getting thinner and thinner. As the hydraulic door check seemed to close the valve on the reservoir of light that filled the corridor, *I'm outta here? Well alrigh*t! I thought jubilantly. After realizing my hospital stay was over, *pack up? Get dressed is more like it*, I chuckled softly to myself while conscious of the fact that I arrived here in my birthday suit. As I lay listening to the early birds revealing to each other their locations in the twilight of the dawn. *Change*, I thought. Change was always something to look forward to. It was always confirming to me that time was passing and my prison sentence was getting shorter. It was customary procedure for an infirmed inmate, once treated, to be returned to their regular quarters where all of their belongings remained untouched. I was returning to building number twenty-two or going home as it's referred to by some inmates anytime one's on their way back to their cell or cube.

Click. I heard the doorknob, this time. "Six o'clock, Zero-two-one-two. The doctor will be here in an hour," she said loudly.

"Check-out time already?" I said jokingly.

"Yep!" she responded, and I watched the wall of light again fade to a thin white line and disappear with the click of the latch bolt. As I lay in the dark silence of my room, thoughts of being back in *g-pop* (general population) left me with the unsettling feeling of knowing that I was returning to the belly of the beast, or back into a hostile environment. After thinking of how nice it would be, to again see the now familiar faces of newfound friends and to get back to work in the free world, outside the gate... I quickly got over it. *I need clothes*, I thought.

I had been wearing flannel pajamas for a month and was pretty much looking forward to receiving a new pair of state greens as promised by Dr Mitchell the second day after my arrival. My old ones were ruined by the blood of the dog. I sat up on my bed, and through the half-raised window to my room, I could see the changing of the guards as I did every morning at this time. A short distance away just beyond the rear entrance to the infirmary, I could see how they were buzzed in and out of the jail by way of the administration building. Jailers' keys, one could never forget the sound of jailers' keys after listening to them for a month as the guards paced in and out, keys jingling at their waists as they changed shifts.

Along with the guards, every now and then, the figures of civilians would appear along the short, concrete walkway. The infirmary staff, program instructors, and the facility's head cook all used the same entrance as the guards. As I sat looking at the parade of facility workers changing shifts in the advancing daylight, I watched enthusiastically awaiting the sight of Dr Mitchell. Pit, pat, pit, pat, went the familiar sound of the heels of his burgundy-colored penny loafers on the concrete as he strode leisurely into the prison compound.

Hurry up!" I said in a low voice hoping the doctor would quicken his pace.

I was hoping to get back to my dorm before morning movement, and only Dr Mitchell could authorize my release from the infirmary in the medical building. I watched him from my second-floor window till he disappeared into the rear entrance way of the infirmary. Ten minutes later...Click.

"Good Morning," said the doctor.

"Morning," I replied.

"Did the nurse tell you?" he asked.

"Yeah, do you think I could make it to morning *chow* at the mess hall?" I asked.

"Sure, if you hurry," he said. "But first let me check

your vitals. Open," he said as his hand reached toward my mouth holding a disposable thermometer.

He strapped me up to a portable blood pressure monitor and squeezed the ball till the strap tightened around my arm. With his stethoscope held in the pit of my elbow, "No working out in the weight yard for a month," he said as he peered at me over the rim of his glasses.

I nodded, *yes.*

"I'm gonna send for you in two weeks to see how you're coming along. If you have any problems drop me a slip," he said and he released the pressure in the strap. 110 over 75, that's normal. Make a fist and hold it for as long as you can," he said, and for the first time in a month, I could close my right hand loosely with little or no pain at all.

"Hurt?" he asked.

I shook my head, *no.*

"Let me see your arm," he said, and I raised my left arm for him to see. "Looks good, looks good," he said and reached for the thermometer I held in my mouth. "I didn't forget your greens. The state shop opens in five minutes – give this referral to the clerk," he said, and he handed me the slip. "You're free to go. I'll call downstairs and let the guard know you're leaving in your pajamas."

"Thanks Doc," I replied, and he walked out.

For the first time in a month, I tied the laces of my boots. As I walked along the deserted walkway toward the state shop, I realized they were too tight, and I stopped to loosen them. When I started walking again, I noticed a guard in the guard post at the next turn. As I neared it, he stepped out.

"What are you, sleepwalking? Where are you coming from?" he asked indignantly.

"The infirmary," I said, and before he asked for it, I handed him my ID card and the referral slip I got from Dr Mitchell.

After he read the referral slip, he said, "The state shop just opened up. Hurry up, before the *chow movement* starts."

He handed back my ID card and the referral. I turned to walk away.

"Wait up! What's in your boots?" he asked.

"Nothin'," I replied.

He had seen me adjust my laces and was just doing his job. Without saying a word, he gestured with his hand, asking for my boots.

"Jail," I said softly, and shook my head in frustration.

While standing barefoot, I remembered the words Hassan said to the group just before the dogs were turned loose: "We put ourselves here, and ain't nobody else's fault but our own."

I thought for a moment…I won't have to do this twice; nothing is worth this humiliation. *Jail was never meant to be a nice place. Unfortunately, some people become institutionalized, complacent and conditioned to this way of life. There's more to life than three hots and a cot or having a full belly and a place to sleep, especially if one must risk his or her own life to do so. Fortunately, jail hasn't much more to offer, so not many people are knocking down the doors trying to get in.*

Upon arriving at the state shop, I was met at the entrance door by the guard on duty. He was standing in the entrance way, sweeping the dirt from the previous day's traffic out onto the pavement.

"Let me guess!" he said, with a surprised look on his face as he held the broom standing in the doorway, "You're here for the Jenny Jones makeover, right?" He laughed. "Man, what are you doing out here in your PJ's? What happened to your clothes," he asked.

"My dog ate 'em," I said with a hint of sarcasm.

"Your dog?" he exclaimed.

"It's a long story. Here," I said, and I handed him the referral with my ID card.

"What are you, just being released from the infirmary?" he asked while looking at the paper. He then leaned the broom against the wall and stepped to the side. "Come on in before somebody sees you and radios in that we have an escapee on the loose over here. Some of these new guys will rush over here, then stand around for fifteen minutes, smoking cigarettes like its break time. It's bad enough I'd have to breathe all that foul air, but then they'd leave their butts all over my dam floors." he said.

The state shop is where inmates are reissued clothing and boots in exchange for old ones. It is where inmates also receive, upon request, three pairs of socks and three pairs of underwear, once every six months. The state shop also darns and mends tattered state-issued clothing and it is up to the guard on duty to determine whether an inmate receive new or used, depending on what's in stock. As I stepped in, I noticed on his desk were four pencils freshly sharpened and lined up perfectly straight alongside the sign in sheet. I signed in, then neatly replaced the pencil. Everywhere you go in jail you must sign in and out. There were signs on all four walls saying: *Sign in, sit down and shut up.* Short legged wooden benches lined the walls and even they had been lined up perfectly straight. I noticed this officer wore a tie and had ironed creases on his shirt, two in front and three in back. His pants were also sharply creased, and he wore black patent leather shoes. You could tell he took pride in being a cop and he obviously ran a tight ship.

"Looking sharp there, man," I said as he walked away.

As he opened the steel door to the large room where all the supplies were kept.

"Yeah, gotta' keep the morale up, you know what I mean?" he said and closed the door behind him.

To the left of the door was a large, screened opening, with a steel counter that ran its length.

As he approached the counter from inside the large room and faced me, "Step back a little," he said. I took two small steps back. Tiptoeing with his elbows on the counter, sizing me up, he said, "Let me guess, large pants, extra-large shirt, am I right?" he asked.

"Yeah, you right," I said.

"Damn, I'm good!" he said and chuckled as he turned and walked away briskly rubbing his palms together. While reaching up to a shelf lined with folded pairs of used pants, he said, "Every year at the Orchid Park Fair, I guess people's weights. My booth always makes the most money. Oh, they love me over there. I've been guessin' weights fourteen years running. They won't let anyone else do it. They all wonder how I'm so good. I won't tell 'em I get a lotta' practice off you guys over here."

"Practice, huh? I replied. *This guy should be on Andy*

of Mayberry, I thought as he searched through a rack of used shirts.

"Hmmm, no extra-large," he said. "Tell you what I'm gonna do, you look like a nice fella, I'm gonna give you a Sunday-go-to-meeting."

"A what?" I asked.

"A brand-new suit. Something you can look good in at holy mass on Sundays," he said as he placed the pair of used pants back on the shelf. He then disappeared behind a wall of shelves and came back with a new pair of pants and a new shirt.

"You think I could change here?" I asked.

"Sure, go ahead," he said, and I quickly slipped out of the pajamas and into the greens. "Hey! Think fast," said the officer from behind.

I turned my head in time to see him toss me a new pair of socks he had rolled together. I thanked him as I sat down on one of the benches to put on the socks.

"Clothes make the man," he said as he shut the steel door behind him. After tying my boots, "Here, stand up! Let me get a good look at you," he said while reaching out for my hand to help me up from the bench. "Put a spit-shine on those leathers and you'll look like a real gentleman," he said, turning me around by the shoulders.

I allowed this officer to take the liberty of having familiarity with me. He seemed genuinely concerned and helpful, and so I addressed him by his name, which I read on his name pin. "Thank you, Officer Smith, you've been quite helpful. I appreciate it," I said and reached out to shake his hand.

As we shook hands, his grip was obviously firm and

genuine. He then clasped my hand between his, and as we stood there, man-to-man, "You know," he started, "it's a shame how so many of your people are winding up in these jails. I'm from the city too you know. I used to live just on the other side of the Brooklyn Bridge, off Atlantic Avenue." He released my hand and folded his arms, "I can remember in the old days walking across the Brooklyn Bridge on Sundays, clear up to Forty-second Street to watch the movies and eat two-for-a-quarter hamburgers at Grant's Restaurant. It wasn't so bad then – what happened? We had our beers, sometimes we even smoked a little pot every now and then. There was never a real problem with drugs. I've lived up here thirty-two years now and I'm retiring soon and from what I hear and see on the news about the city, it scares me. I wouldn't set foot back there for all the tea in China. I did hope for some day to be moving back but it seems like I'll be spending out the rest of mine right up here. These hillbillies ain't so bad once you get used to 'em, and they're a hell of a lot safer to live around," he said.

"Hmmm," was all I could say to that.

Actually, I could have said more but I wanted to end the conversation right there. I wanted to get to my dorm, go to *chow* and then go to work. Plus, I concluded that even if I spent all day talking to Officer Smith, I couldn't undo in a day, what he spent at least thirty-two years justifiably, according to him, doing to himself. I could have told him that, *If you're not part of the solution, you're probably part of the problem and that white flight never solved anything so you should have stuck around the city to help resolve your neighborhood's conflicts. And maybe if you weren't so*

89

busy smoking pot, every now and then, the city's pervasive drug problem may have never come to fruition. Or I could have just asked him: *Safer to live around than who?* Then tossed him his socks back. The guilt would have probably sent him to an early grave, so I kept my opinion to myself.

"OK, you'd better get to *chow.* Don't worry, I'll sign you out," he said.

"Thanks again," I said, and left.

Stepping out of the state shop, I noticed the *chow* movement was under way. The mess hall was between the state shop and my destination, building number twenty-two. I could see inmates filing out of two of the four buildings across from building twenty-two and coming towards me, headed for the mess hall. The sun was just above the horizon and the pale blue sky, without a cloud to be seen, hinted of another glorious day in the making. I took a deep breath through my nose, and I could smell the clean freshness of fermenting grass left behind from yesterday's cut by the inside lawns and grounds crew. The wide-open space of the sprawling prison grounds, excavated into the low plateau on which Mohawk was erected, was dwarfed by the hills, fields and valleys of the majestic mountains surrounding it.

I love it, but I can't wait to leave it, I thought. Under my own accord, yeah, but not as a prisoner, not like Officer Smith anyway. I then felt the inner peace and calmness inside me that mornings like this always seemed to affect. But unlike the free world, outside the gate, that feeling of inner peace never lasted long enough.

While passing the mess hall, I heard, "Hey *akh!*" greeted by an inmate as we passed.

"Awww man, you back on a violation? Aw man, that's bad, that's bad, *akhi*," he repeated before I could answer him.

He assumed I was released, went home, then violated my parole as happens to more than just a few repeat offenders. I was out of general population for a month, and he like all others, just hadn't seen me. The mere fact that one is recognized as having been absent, usually means that person had been released and returned to prison on a violation of parole. The present system handles parole violations in such a manner as to return individuals to the facility from which they were paroled. My assessment of this is that it is meant to cause embarrassment to the inmate, hoping to create lasting rehabilitation. What this inmate said caught me off guard and seeing the disdainful looks on the faces of other passers-by, I felt I wanted to yell to him the true explanation for my absence. You're not allowed to change direction or deviate from your destination, or even stop on the walkway and so as we gained more distance from each other, I decided to leave well enough alone and leave him with his preconceived thoughts.

As I continued toward building twenty-two or the *projects*, so nicknamed by the inmates because unlike the other dormitories in the compound, it was three stories tall instead of one. I glanced over my shoulder at the spot in front of the mess hall where the two officers that were beaten a month ago lay motionless, and seemingly lifeless. I then scanned the field of grass that lay between the mess hall, building twenty-two and the four smaller dorms across the way. It was so perfectly manicured that it was hard to believe that only a short while ago, inhumane acts of terror and death were carried out on this beautiful lawn which posed as the stage in this wasteland of social misfits.

Upon entering the lobby of building twenty-two, there was no feeling of exhilaration as one gets sometimes after finally returning home after a long trip. Though there are a few times you may experience joy in a given situation while behind bars, returning to your cube or cell is like returning a canary to its cage: although it can be happy at times, true happiness lies in its freedom. I descended the stairs and approached the locked door to my dormitory. As I peered through the thick, metal-reinforced, glass window, I could see most of the residents, my dorm mates, were grouped near the door awaiting the *chow call*. I heard the phone ring at the desk and saw the guard on duty slowly walk out of the TV room. He was watching the morning news and stopped to answer it.

"Home sweet home," I said facetiously when I realized it was the same creep guard who tried to write me a ticket months earlier for having milk on my windowsill.

He was still keeping up good form, true to his better-than-thou character that he consistently portrayed while on duty. *I'd like to bust this punk up one day*, I thought, then asked for Allah's forgiveness for having such ill thoughts. It was very irritating to see some guards portray the mister tough guy image. Not to say that prison guards are not tough, but watching this guy being treated like a rookie by his peers months back, I knew he wasn't as thick-skinned as he tried to make himself appear. I think it's probably fear and ignorance that drives men like these to take lightly the mental attitude of confined, convicted felons. Some of which who while on the streets, have killed at the drop of a hat, or the bat of an eye, or to put food in their stomachs such as they were waiting to do now. As he hung up the phone, he taunted the inmates who were waiting in anticipation for a confirmation by phone from the mess hall. It was to let them know as to whether or not it was their house's turn for *chow*.

"That was my travel agent," he said, with a smirk on his face.

As he folded his arms and leaned back on the desk, he continued, "He said I can stop by and pick up my round-trip tickets and hotel reservations for my trip to Aruba. Any of you guys wanna come?" he said and laughed.

"Ah man, stop fuckin around, is it *chow*, or not?" said one inmate very angrily.

He was leaning on the Plexiglass partition that separated the TV room from the main dorm.

"It's *chow* when I say it's *chow*," snapped the guard. He then unfolded his arms, stood up, and slowly walked around the desk. As he picked up the mic to the intercom, he reached in his pocket for a handkerchief, "This thing is filthy," he said, and he proceeded to wipe the microphone with it. He then put the microphone back on the desk, looked at the now frustrated inmates and asked, "What?" then said, "Oh yeah!" and picked up the mic again and shouted into it, "*On the chow!*" As he walked toward the door to unlock it, he noticed me through the window on the other side. "Well, well, look who's back," he said while stepping to the side. "You're too late, we've already fed the dog," he said sarcastically, then burst into laughter. It was a cruel thing to say to someone who had just spent a month in the hospital suffering from a dog attack.

"Dog food, I'ma call you dog food from now on," he said to me as I walked past him.

"Good! Then you can call your momma over and let the bitch eat me," I retorted.

The whole dorm exploded into laughter and from the look on this officer's face he regretted leaving himself open for the embarrassment. I was welcomed with genuine greetings and handshakes by my dormmates.

"We thought you was dead Bilal," said Woody after waiting turns to greet me.

"Dead?" I repeated, "It's gonna take a lot more than guard dogs to take me off the count, or even guards for that matter," I boasted loudly while making eye contact with the guard who was now sitting at the desk.

I did this intentionally to irritate this guard as a form of payback or giving him a dose of his own medicine. Perhaps the embarrassment would make him a better person, but hopefully it would teach him that he was out of his league when it came to trying to intimidate me in public. As I said earlier, he was a country boy, and I was... well, you know the rest.

As my dormmates were leaving for *chow*, I found myself obstructing their path, and I stepped to the side, facing the Plexiglass window to the TV room. A familiar face flashed across the TV screen momentarily and now the focus of my attention was solely upon it. It was the morning news broadcast, and they were showing the footage of a crime scene with paramedics removing a covered body on a stretcher from a pub in downtown Manhattan. I was on the other side of the Plexiglass partition and couldn't hear the broadcast. I hurried inside hoping for another glimpse on the screen of the person that I couldn't readily identify.

"Peterson was shot to death by bar owner Thomas O'Riley after leaving O'Riley left for dead behind the bar with two bullet wounds to O'Riley's abdomen," the broadcaster said as I entered the TV room. "Sources say that Peterson, recently paroled from prison in upstate New York, had a history of armed robberies dating back twelve years. "Back to the studio," he said as he ended the broadcast.

I was left in deep thought trying to make a connection with the face I saw on the screen and the name: Peterson.

"Peterson," I repeated to myself then it flashed in my mind the name Ronald Peterson and now the face had a name. "Musa!" I said loudly.

I couldn't believe it. At first it just didn't register until I slowly rehashed the broadcast and all I knew presently of Musa. It finally dawned on me that he got an open release date for the fifth of this month and now this month was in its last week. *Musa went home*, I thought, and at that instant the broadcast became a corroborant to that fact. It all added up. Musa was doing time for armed robbery the last time I saw him. I felt an emptiness in the pit of my stomach, my appetite was completely gone. The thought of never seeing Musa again, had never occurred to me. We had even exchanged phone numbers so we could contact each other when we were both released. Now we, like many other friends and family I've known in the past, would have to wait till the day of judgement before we would ever cross paths again, if at all. Some people are born losers and Musa unfortunately was a perfect example...

I left the TV room and headed for my cube. As I entered my semiprivate room, I found Rico fast asleep but fully dressed lying face down on his bunk. Mr. Watts was sitting on his bunk yawning, and in the middle of a stretch, with both arms extended over his head. He wasn't aware of my presence, so I waited till he lowered his arms. In jail, little things mean a lot and something as small as a good stretch may be the only motivation one gets not to despair but to keep putting the days behind them.

"Don't be getting too comfortable back here. You know boss man don't wanna see us too happy," I said jokingly.

"My man!" exclaimed Mr. Watts as he stood up after me surprising him. "My main man! How you doin', boy? Rico said he saw you sittin' in the grass after they called them damn dogs off. I didn't believe 'em after what I seen one of them dogs do to a guy right next to me, ripped his goddamn throat out. I thought you was dead boy but thank God you alright. There is a Jesus, you know. Don't let nobody tell you there ain't no Jesus," he said while looking me in the eyes very concernedly.

"I said I was a Muslim, not a Jew...We believe in Jesus, Mr. Watts but that's another story," I said while stepping into my cubicle, "So, tell me, how've you been?"

"Oh, my arthritis kicks up every now and then, but outside of that, the old man's doing alright. How you been, son? Or let me start with, where you been?" said Watts inquisitively.

Well needless to say, I missed *chow* while Watts

brought me up to speed on the latest goings on of our dormmates. I told him about the microsurgery they performed to reattach the severed veins in my left arm. During my stay at the infirmary, my boots served as my slippers, and I decided to give them a well-deserved shine. As Watts and I talked, I sat on my bunk doing just that. I heard Rico stirring in his bunk.

Suddenly, "Bilal, haha, Bilal," he said, and I heard him rushing over to greet me.

I got a good feeling inside the moment I saw him. I thought about the courageous way he grouped his forces on the day of the dogs and how, because of the stand he and his men took, the rest of the inmates followed suit and joined forces with the Muslims. It was a brave thing to do but of course, maybe if he hadn't, the inmates would not have seemed so formidable and threatening and the guards may never had turned the dogs loose, though I wouldn't stake my life on it. I stood up to greet him. We shook hands and embraced each other like brothers.

"You kill that dog, I see you kill that fucking dog," he said with his heavy Puerto Rican accent. "How you do that? Man!" he said with astonishment.

"Rico," I said, "I wanna thank you for helping us that day."

Rico responded, "I see you pray all the time. You good man, you have good friends. I watch you Bilal. Some Muslims fulla shit, they make fights, they fucking up, this no good. You think I no see? I see... You good man, Bilal," he said convincingly. Rico paused, "Plus you my roomie, I watch you back, you watch mine," he said and smiled.

Just then, Woody came back from *chow*. "OK, break

it up, break it up," he said as he entered. "What's this, a union meeting?" he asked jokingly. "Without me?" he said while standing in the entry way to my cubicle gesturing for a hug. "Come on, gimme love Bilal, gimme love," he said.

I stood up and gave him a back patting hug, all the while repeating jokingly, "Poor little baby, poor, little baby."

Give the man some air," said Watts, "He don't want you smotherin' him all to death."

"Oh Watts, chill," said Woody. "You just jealous cause don't nobody wanna hug you," he said.

"I don't need no hugs," said Watts. "I'm a man," he added.

"Aw man," said Woody and waved his hand at Watts, shooing him away. "What's this I hear about you killin' dogs and shit?" said Woody.

"Slapped that monkey right outta' his tree," I said smilingly. "Broke his dam jaw," I boasted. Then I explained to the three of them how I killed the dog.

"Damn!" said Woody. "You lucky man, that damn dog coulda killed you," he said.

Woody was right – that dog could have killed me... As the four of us stood there talking, I found myself answering their questions in between my thoughts of how these three men were obviously showing a true fondness of me. We were all from different walks of life, but we all had a common bond, we were outcasts of society and as Rico said, we were roomies. As funny as it sounds, it felt good to be back. We chatted a few minutes more, waiting for the programs movement to begin.

"Oh, I almost forgot!" said Woody. "Your mail, Bilal, I've been holdin' your mail," he said and turned to get it from his locker.

"Mail? I got mail?" I said.

"Yeah, I figured you had to come back home sometime and ain't no tellin' what these fool cops woulda done with it if nobody grabbed it at mail call."

Woody handed me three letters. My excitement waned quickly when I realized none were from home. *Home, oh how I wished this were all behind me,* I thought. The first day passed uneventfully— it was like the world hadn't missed me at all. After all, who was I to think that maybe I could have somehow left an indelible mark on this society that would affect a profound change in my absence, enough to recognize that their hero has returned? The humdrum routine of prison life quickly welcomed me with open arms, embracing me as just another one of its foster children who fell out of cadence during their march into infinity. By the following day, it was like I never left at all. My hospital stay was just a fading memory that the daily routine of life behind bars quickly erased from my mind. Now, between my job and the other programs prescribed by my counselor, there left little time to dwell on such things as trivial as the niceties I left behind in the infirmary. Simple things like sitting in the window for hours on end watching the clouds pass or the coaxing of red squirrels from a nearby tree to my windowsill by slipping pieces of bread and fruit through the bars. Relatively speaking, the infirmary was a picnic, but now I was back in jail.

CHAPTER 4

T.O.S.

A little more than a week had gone by and Alim and I spoke often at *chow* of how strange it was to not have Musa joining us at our table. Alim made mention of how he and Musa once had the same conversation about me when I was hospitalized. He spoke of how they routinely guarded against any newcomer or even veteran inmate from sitting in my usual seat, such as the way we now honored the memory of Musa in his absence. One day started out as usual, with Alim and I eating morning *chow* and returning to our separate dorms. Then as our regular routine, we were to meet in front of building twenty-two when the programs movement started. Due to unforeseen circumstances, Alim never showed, and I subsequently left for the east end of the compound without him. I was on my way to work and had spent enough time slow walking, trying to wait for Alim to catch up. I had already passed the mess hall, the state shop and the medical building. Now coming upon a guard post at the next turn, it was time for me to walk at a normal speed, or at least at the same pace as the other inmates. By now they had crowded the walkway for as far as I could see, in front and behind me. Stragglers were either verbally reprimanded or written-up and served a summons that if found guilty at an appointed hearing, would be penalized with facility service work without pay. Or worse, fined, having the penalty monetarily deducted from their commissary account. I was already indigent as it was, and a deduction from my account would have left me without enough funds to buy my bi-weekly supply of postage stamps. I quickened my pace and gave up all hopes of Alim ever catching up. As I rounded the turn while passing the guard post, I noticed it was empty. I could see down the hill, the east gate and tower and the programs building one hundred yards to the right of it. I was headed for the east gate where I normally, before starting work, met the outside lawns and grounds crew consisting of four men, myself included. In the distance, I could make out the figures of three men, my crew standing at the base of the watch tower next to the gate, and two guards standing on the catwalk that surrounded it above them.

The thick line of inmates surrounding me all wearing green state issued garb filled the walkway from curb to curb, all filing into the programs building at the bottom of the hill. A few were instructors but most were students and trade apprentices. I noticed a lone inmate at the bottom of the hill who parted from the crowd and veered left walking along the east gate walkway toward the three men at the base of the tower. This guy's going to get a ticket, I thought. Unless they hired a new man? I questioned. The outside lawns and grounds crew was shorthanded.

Although we made it through the previous winter with only a four-man crew, I dreaded the thought of having to repeat the drudgery of plowing snow next winter in below freezing temperatures for seven hours a day with little or no relief because of the lack of experienced drivers. I hoped this lone inmate on the east gate walkway was a new member of the crew, better yet, a new member of the crew with a driver's license. Even an expired one would be valid here.

As the dense crowd negotiated the turn, now some twenty yards behind me, I suddenly heard, "*Allahu Akbar, Allahu Akbar!*" being yelled in a frantic voice behind me.

It was a Muslim's cry for help, his way of getting the attention of any Muslims within earshot that could help him. No sooner than I could turn toward the screams, I was knocked to the ground by the force of the exploding crowd as inmates tried to distance themselves from an attack or hit in progress. I laid prone and covered my head with my hands, all the while knowing they served as little protection from the state-issued workman's boots worn by most of the inmates as they swished past my face too close for comfort. I heard the voice cry out again repeating, "*Allahu Akbar!*" this time slightly muffled, indicating to me that the victim was covering up, protecting himself from his attackers.

There was no guard in the small guard house, and it seemed as if whoever was attacking did so while taking advantage of this fact. It was a perfect location for a *rub-out* or hit also known as a *TOS* (terminate on site). I heard steel shanks and bangers hitting the pavement as inmates who had nothing to do with the incident dropped their concealed weapons whilst fleeing the area. They knew the routine of everyone being searched by the guards immediately on the spot after a hit. I lifted my head thinking the coast was clear to take a look in the direction of the scuffle. Suddenly, I saw stars when I was accidentally kicked in the head by an inmate who jumped over me as he ran from the scene. I covered up again, holding my head to relieve the pain and feel the area where I was kicked, checking for blood. It was a relief to find only an enlarging bump with no broken skin. I now lay on my side and noticed I was seeing double from the impact.

"*Allahu Akbar, Allahu Akbar!*" I heard in a desperate voice closer this time and I feared this Muslim was beyond help unless I could regain my faculties.

I strained to focus on an object on the ground only two feet in front of me. To my surprise, it was a foot-long piece of sharpened pencil rod steel dropped by a fleeing inmate. It was neatly wrapped with electrical tape on one end that served as its handle for it to be used as a puncture weapon. It reminded me of an extra-large ice pick. Now more than anything else, I wanted to get as far away from it as I possibly could. I didn't need to do six months in the box for a weapon that wasn't mine. I could hear the heavy thud of body punches being delivered by what had to be a very large or very strong man. It was close, so close I could hear the breath of the attackers and the grunts of their victim as they struggled with one another. Still seeing double, though feeling it was safe to do so, I sat up to see two Hispanic inmates kneeling over what was obviously a Muslim wearing a white *kufi*.

The Muslim was a new transfer from another

correctional facility, Abdul Latiff (La-teef). Latiff had just been transferred to Mohawk on the previous Friday. I remembered him introducing himself at *Jummah* and explaining to the community that he had been in an altercation with another inmate at Clinton Correctional Facility in Dannemora, NY where the inmate died of multiple stab wounds from his own weapon and that he was transferred here to avoid retaliation by the inmates' friends. Latiff went on to explain how he was acquitted of the charge of manslaughter and the death of the inmate was found to be caused by Lattif, in self-defense. That inmate was a Latin King, gang banger, and now it seemed pretty obvious that Latiff had a reputation in his following. News travels fast throughout the prison systems, with the transferring of inmates from jail to jail. Numerous incidences of mistaken identity occur amongst inmates, especially when one inmate is bitter and seeking revenge. With time on their hands and despair in their hearts, anger can brood in the soul of a man, causing him to lash out at the wrong person with deadly vengeance disregarding the consequences. Evidently someone identified Latiff as that man from Clinton, but this time unmistakably, they had their man.

As the two gangbangers knelt over Latiff, I could see that one inmate had his back to me and was obviously a body builder. He was on one knee holding Latiff by the throat with one hand and repeatedly dropping bombshell-like punches into Latiff's head and face. The other, a smaller man, was on the opposite side with a flat-honed shank in one hand and hesitantly awaiting an opportunity to reach in with this edged weapon and slice at Latiff's arms and torso. It was a sloppy assault, fortunately for Latiff because it could have been worse if the big guy wasn't in the way. Suddenly the big guy stopped punching, and from the way he quickly looked around, I knew he had made plans to change his course of attack. He reached back and held his hand over his back pocket then hesitated, first quickly looking left, then right. I strained to focus and for a split second I could clearly see steel in the pocket below his hand and knew this guy was going all the way. As he grabbed the shank and fully exposed it, holding it behind his back, looking for an opportunity to finalize this ill deed…

"*Allahu Akbar!*" I yelled from less than ten feet away.

It stopped him dead in his tracks. Now the big guy focused his attention on me. As he snapped his head around. The look of surprise on his face quickly turned to anger the instant he realized he had two Muslims to contend with. Now his anger turned to a fiendish grin as he turned facing me, shank in hand with the look of a crazed killer. Somehow, I felt this guy wasn't new to this. Squatting and facing me, it must have looked to him as if I were a helpless sacrificial lamb set out for slaughter, sitting there waiting to be bled and gutted. As I sat on the pavement anticipating his next move, inmates were still scrambling from the scene. I looked at the shank in his hand and shuddered at the sight of the amount of flat pointed steel that extend from its handle. It was long enough to pass completely through my body. My life at this point was in danger and an assault on me next was imminent. The thought of dying in prison was all too real. I wasn't going to just lay down my life and die without a good fight. I thought about my family back home and how they would take the news of my death. I wasn't a jail bird. Yeah, I made a few mistakes in my life but none of them punishable by death, certainly not like this. I had never done a state bid before this one. In fact, this was my first arrest as an adult. *How did I wind up here?* I thought to myself.

He motioned toward me and in his eyes, I read death. The adrenalin surged through my veins, and I could feel every cell in my body come to life.

The nerve of this punk, I thought. *Hurt me?* I recall saying to myself.

He lunged at me springing catlike with his weapon held high, attempting to deprive me of the balance of the only life Allah had blessed me with. *The steel*, I thought. I remembered the weapon dropped near my head by a running inmate only moments earlier. I groped for the weapon on the ground behind me, never taking my eyes off his shank held high as he lunged closer. My hand found the taped handle without a split second to spare. As he came down plunging hard with his weapon, I was already focused intently on the path it was taking toward my body. Nothing on Earth had ever gotten my attention as much, before or since, as that shank and the body that was attached to it. I grabbed his wrist with my free hand and felt the cold steel of his blade press hard against my forearm as the weight of his body carried us both toward the pavement. All I could think of at that instant was, *you had your chance and now it's my turn.*

Instinctively, I swung hard, curling my arm, guiding the steel home deep into his vitals. The steel rod penetrated his body with surprisingly little effort. The only resistance I felt was when the pointed tip of my weapon encountered his ribs and then glanced off slipping between two of them. I was flat on my back holding his upper body suspended above me. My left hand still gripping his wrist holding the shank at bay and my right hand firmly attached to the handle of my weapon, which seemed to be buried deep in his heart. It was like I had a hold on the pulse of life itself as he hung there, now trembling uncontrollably. I pushed him back onto his knees. He didn't resist, but the pressure of his grip on the shank told me this man still had enough life in his body to put me away for good and that he was still too dangerous to let go. I was scared, scared of what his partner, whom I couldn't see, might do next. Scared of letting this man go, fearing he might kill me, I knew I was the underdog. I was flat on my back and here was a man kneeling over me with a knife who outweighed me by fifty pounds. My dilemma caused me to just go for broke and not waste time on consequential thinking. I had to end this quick...

I yanked the steel from his body and heard a short whoosh of air, like when one relaxes their pinch on the neck of a balloon. It was air from his lungs escaping through his body cavity when I retracted the weapon. Still feeling that my life was at threat and not feeling secure in whether this man was completely debilitated, I cocked my arm quickly and in one wide sweep, I aimed as high as I could and let fly. When this inmate didn't blink an eye as the tool passed completely through his neck, I knew he was dead on his feet, or knees to be exact. He didn't even react. He just knelt there trembling, eyes bulging in a gawking stare, looking as if he were about to vomit. I relaxed my grip on his wrist and with reflex speed I tightened it again, checking to see if my prognosis of this would-be killer was correct. There was no change.

He's dead, I surmised, and now and only now I felt safe and secure enough in my decision to let him go. I released his wrist, still holding on to the trembling shaft through his neck not yet fully ready to give up complete control of this situation. As I propped myself up from the pavement with my free hand, I pushed myself away from him, simultaneously slipping the tool from his neck. It was a weird sight, to see this inmate kneeling there, with knife in hand, trembling, and his face masked in an unmistakable expression of death. I quickly rose to my feet and caught a glimpse from behind of the partner of this transgressor deceased, hightailing it into the crowd.

As I was leaving the scene, I turned, to visually check the condition of my Muslim brother. At this point, although I didn't want to, I had to make the rational decision to let go and let God handle the outcome of Latiff's situation. I had just killed a man, and this wasn't like in the war where it was your job and sanctioned by the government. Although it was justifiably so, when you are a ward of the state, incarcerated and commit a homicide, you may as well be tried in a kangaroo court because it's a good possibility you will be railroaded or charged and convicted in the first degree and given the maximum sentence, as a rule.

Latiff was now standing on solid ground, obviously in some pain and badly shaken, but standing. He seemed to have more concern for me than he did for his own wounds that were bleeding profusely from his right arm which he cradled with his left hand. As our eyes made contact, he smiled a weak smile then strained with his left hand to lift his blood-soaked right arm. He managed to squeeze out of his right hand a blood drenched fist with the index finger pointed skyward. He was signaling as Muslims often do, implying, there is only one God. It was picture perfect and this scene could have been used on a poster as a symbol for *jihad* (war), battle-worn and bloodied as he was.

In the days of the Prophet Muhammad, those who waged wars against Allah and his messenger had to contend with Muslims who believed then and now, that to die in the cause of Allah and the spread of Islam would reap them great rewards in the Hereafter and woe was it to those who transgressed on Muslims and brought about jihad upon themselves.

Quran, 5:33 The punishment of those who wage war against Allah (swt) and his messenger and strive with might and main for mischief through the land is execution or crucifixion or the cutting off of hands and feet from opposite sides, or exile from the land. That is their disgrace in this world and a heavy punishment is theirs in the Hereafter.

As Latiff stood there bloodied and battle-worn, his head donned in a now blood-spattered, white *kufi*, holding up his now wavering symbol, he uttered to me the words, "*La ilaha illallah* (there is no deity but Allah)."

I gave him a quick nod of my head and said, "*Assalamu alaikum, akhi.*"

"*Walaikum salaam,*" I heard him reply, as I turned and broke into a quick sprint and caught up with the fleeing crowd.

Now well-blended, I heard those unmistakable jailer's keys coming toward me getting nearer and nearer till the sound of the jingle raised my pulse rate almost to its limit. I felt my heart in my throat when the first guard paralleled my position on the walkway. He was running at full steam towards Latiff and the dead man behind me. It wasn't until the third or fourth running guard passed me by, that I felt somewhat assured that I had in fact escaped unseen. *Could it be true, that I would be unidentified as the inmate who bestowed wrath on the figure now lying face down with both hands at his sides? He was lying in what seemed from that distance to be a small pool of blood around the head-shoulder area.*

I made my way through the crowd with the shank tucked up my right sleeve, holding on to it for dear life, all the while knowing only my prints on the weapon could tie me to the body. Unravelling the tape from the shaft, as I was headed pushing and shoving hell-bent for the east gate walkway, I noticed a manhole in the center of the walkway. I paused, then side stepped and made my way through the crowd to its vented cover, reached down and let the shaft slip through one of the vent holes. The sound of the shaft slightly brushing against the sides of the vent hole caused it to make a ringing sound, like a tuning fork does when struck with metal. I could hear it ringing as it quickly faded away to a squelch. At that point, I felt with the weapon now underwater, it was hidden far from sight, well enough for me to ever have to worry about anyone ever seeing it again. I rolled the black gummy tape between both palms into a ball and as I approached the fork in the walkway, I let it drop to the ground at my side and departed from the crowd. I walked at a quick pace down the east gate walkway up to the now four men standing at the base of the watch tower. I was in deep thought over the incident that had just taken place and hadn't noticed our new teammate.

Suddenly I was greeted with, "*Assalamu alaikum, akh.*"

Instinctively responding with, "*Walaikum salaam,*" I looked toward my greeter and to my surprise it was Mel, my old roomie. I must have looked to everyone present, my crew, as if I had just seen a ghost, standing there with my mouth agape and my eyes opened wide.

"What the fuck happened up the hill?" he asked. I was still aghast with my mouth still wide open. "What happened on the hill, *akh*?" he repeated.

"Huh?" I uttered.

"Helloooo?" said Mitch, as if implying, Is anyone home in there? (Mitch was a fair-minded chap from South Hampton on Long Island New York.) I was stuck or frozen just by seeing Mel to begin with, compounded by seeing him so, what seemed to be out of place. I hadn't seen Mel in three months since he bunked next to me.

"What are you doing here?" I asked Mel.

"I'm on your crew, I work with you guys" he said.

"When did you get out?" I asked.

"I didn't," he replied. "It's a long story, *akh*. I'll tell you about it later."

At that point, I realized that now wasn't the time to discuss in public something as private and as personal as the now touchy subject of suicide. I was overwhelmed by the mere sight of Mel. And although I was anxious to speak with him at length regarding his health and well-being, I had more serious concerns of my own at present to clear up before I could even begin to ponder over questions and statements that I previously prepared and had in store for him if ever again we crossed paths. Two things at this time were of paramount concern: One was to get outside the gate ASAP as to not be of suspect in the death of the dead man on the walkway; and two, was the identity of the creep who got away.

"Good morning, guys," I greeted.

"Good morning," they all repeated, except Mel.

He straightened his back, threw out his chest, and in a somewhat proud and dignified manner, said, "*Walaikum.*"

I stared at him momentarily, then smiled an ever-broadening smile, "Let me find out you clocking my Arabic," I said jokingly, then stepped toward him and embraced him like a brother. It was humorous for me, to hear Mel respond to me greeting him good morning with the Arabic word *walaikum.* I had used the word in response to him greeting me good morning, but in a facetious manner on the morning of the day he attempted to kill himself.

There it was right outside the window, Spring, but it was more like the dead of winter with the windows rattling from a windstorm that was obviously wreaking havoc on all God's creatures that weren't indoors. I had just woken up and was astounded by the winter weather conditions outside. To me, they were not normal for that time of year. In the pre-dawn silence of my dorm, I questioned aloud the statement, It's April?

Mel had overheard me and greeted me with, Good morning! When actually, to me and a lot of other God's creatures, it wasn't. So, trying not to be impolite, I responded with, *Walaikum*, and Mel remembered…It means in Arabic, and upon you too.

"When I grow up, I want to be just like you, Bilal." said Mel laughingly while we embraced.

"If, you grow up," I responded, then stepped back and looked Mel squarely in the eyes and nodded my head implying, you know what I mean.

His laughter turned quickly to a weak smile. Then he tightened his chin to a frown and lowered his eyes momentarily.

"Come on, let's get to work – Where's Officer Diamond?" I said.

"Here he comes now," said Devine.

Devine was a good hearted, hardworking young man of thirty-one years but as athletically active as any twenty-two-year-old— you'd find on any ball court in any one of New York City's numerous pockets of ghetto. He happened to be from Bed Stuy, (Bedford Stuyvesant) in Brooklyn, and had on and off ties with The Nation of Islam, better known as the Black Muslims. As I looked through the fencing wire of the gate itself toward Diamond, he was about to exit the state green van, which was our crew's transportation and utility vehicle. He had just pulled into the trap, the area between the double-gated entrance. He was half in and half out of the driver's door looking up, speaking loudly to the guard above him through the watch tower's intercom system.

Now my heart picked up from where it left off on the walkway. *Something's up!* I thought, *I hope that tower guard didn't see me on the hill.*

"Hey!" yelled Diamond to get our attention, "Who was the last one on the walkway?"

As I stood there breathless, coldly staring at the watch tower, it felt as if my feet were made of lead and now the feeling of hopelessness came over me as my heart sank to the pit of my stomach. *I'm busted*, I said to myself…That instant, I found myself asking God for this whole scene not to be true and if it was, to please let me get off lightly and not have my numeral bid sentence turn into just letters. Or to be exact, do L-I-F-E in prison for someone who had brought death upon themselves. All eyes were on me as I stood there with knitted brow and clenched teeth. I stared intermittently at the tower window, then Diamond, then the window, then Diamond. It seemed as if the whole world got silent as a rush of anger peaked inside me until it seemed to flow through my ears. I was angry, mad as hell over the possibility that now my sentence will be extended and only God knows when I'd get out of prison.

Although my crew members were in prison for various types of crimes the expression *there's honor amongst thieves* now came to mind when I realized no one was pointing a finger or even posturing toward me. Inmates have a way of taking the heat off of their buddies or helping them out of tight situations whenever possible. Being in jail is enough as far as they're concerned. Generally speaking, no matter what their crime, no one wants to see anyone else get in more trouble or have to do hard time while they're already doing time in jail.

"What's it to you?" answered Tony, following a long pause of silence regarding Diamond's question as to who was the last one to come up the east gate walkway.

All brawn and brains, Tony was a state-side born Puerto Rican, thirty-five years old from East Harlem, Spanish Harlem or El Barrio it's known as to native New Yorkers in New York City. Now the moment of truth had come, and I remember feeling this same way the day I got sentenced; standing there in court, obviously guilty, with the jury and a hundred other strangers looking on while the judge asked, Do you have anything to say for yourself? Although stricken by fear of the unknown...

"I was!" I now spoke up, "I was the last one on the walkway." I directed to Diamond.

"The rest of you guys stay put," he said.

As the magnetic click of the locks sounded, the massive gate in front of us rolled slowly open, allowing me entrance into the trap. (A double gated entrance/exit, such as an airlock)

As I approached Diamond, I could hear the gate slowly rolling back until it slammed shut, "What's up?" I asked.

"This guy seems to think you might have seen something on the walkway," he said while looking up at the tower.

Then a tall, muscular guard stepped out of the tower onto the grated catwalk that encircled it. Looking up at him through the gratings wearing his gun belt, carrying a scoped high-power rifle and wearing shooting glasses, led one to believe that this tower guard is no joke.

"What happened up there?" he asked while looking down at me over the waist high railing.

"I don't know, sir," I responded, "The crowd behind me just broke into a panic for some reason and everyone started running down the hill. Us guys up front got pushed from behind, so we had to run or get trampled. Can't you see from up there?" I asked.

"Diamond! Get these guys outta' here, hurry up," he said without responding to my question.

"Gimme the gate," Diamond said to him. "Let's go!" he now directed to the rest of the crew and the magnetically controlled bolts of the huge gate's locks sounded once again, and the four men walked past the rolling gate inside the trap to join Diamond and me. As the last man passed the gate, it shuddered then reversed its direction until it shut closed.

"What happened back there on the hill?" I asked Diamond.

"Beats the shit outta me," he said. "None of you guys saw anything?" he asked.

"Oh, like we'd tell you, cop!" stated Mitch jokingly.

"I heard on my radio it was one of your guys, Tony."

"One of my guys? One of my guys what?" he asked.

"One of your guys is dead up there," said Diamond.

"Dead!" repeated Mitch, Devine and Tony simultaneously.

"Yeah, one of Bilal's guys killed him."

"What!" I exclaimed.

"They said a Muslim killed a Latin King or a Neta on the hill," reported Diamond.

"I ain't no gangbanger," said Tony with a hint of indignation in his voice.

"What makes you think it's a Muslim?" I said.

"They caught a suspect who was wearing a beanie like yours. I even see some white guys wearing beanies, hanging with the Muslims. Are they Muslims too?"

"Yes they are." I stated.

"I don't know, man. All'a you guys are in one gang or another," said Diamond.

"Muslims ain't no gang," said Devine with obvious indignation, "Y'all always trying to stir up some shit. Man, I be glad to get the fuck out this bullshit jail. I can't wait to get transferred to a minimum."

"Minimum? You ain't goin' nowhere till I let you go," Diamond said jokingly.

"I'm getting the fuck outta here," said Devine.

"What! And leave all your buddies here at Mohawk?" said Diamond.

"I ain't got no buddies in Mohawk, I can't wait to get the fuck away from all y'all motha fuckas…Not y'all, and no offense to you, Mitch. Y'all know what I mean," he said.

"Why don't you just say you hate fucking white people?" said Diamond.

"I don't have to, you just did," said Devine.

"Okay! Y'all scaring the new guy," I stated to calm things down a bit.

I still wanted out the other gate. And Diamond and Devine have been known to go on like this for hours.

"Strip!" commanded the gun-toting tower guard.

The mountain air was cold some mornings and this happened to be one of them.

"Oh, come on!" cried Mitch.

"It's cold out here, Diamond," complained Tony.

I was already standing in my stocking feet and ready to unsnap my state pants when Diamond looked up at him through the grating and said, "Give 'em a break, Hargrove. My guys weren't involved."

As he looked down through the grating, his hands were crossed across the rifle, which was cradled in one arm with the barrel pointing upwards. He gave an affirmative salute to Diamond without saying a word, then turned and stepped back inside the tower.

"Come on guys, let's do this quick," said Diamond. We're running late, he said. Because of all the commotion we're not gonna stop at the pantry to pick up any grub today. We've still got plenty of food in the fridge at the shop. he said. And they've got my favorite, devil's food cake, with chocolate frosting for dessert. He added while shaking his head in disappointment.

"Yeah man, that's my favorite too!" exclaimed Mel.

By now everyone was untying their shoelaces.

"We gotta strip?" asked Mel.

"Just your shoes," I replied.

"Leave your socks on and empty your pockets on the bench here," Diamond said and pointed to a long metal bench that ran along the wall at the base of the watch tower. After Diamond patted us down half-heartedly, he turned each pair of boots upside down and slapped the heels together. We then sat one by one as he finished checking them. Next, he went inside the tower to check us off the head count.

"Y'all do this shit every day, *akh*?" Mel asked.

"Times two, on the way out and on the way back in," I replied.

I stood up after tying my laces, and watched through the wire fencing the emergency vehicles up the hill and hoped Latiff was rushed to the infirmary. Suddenly a facility ambulance pulled away from the scene and zig-zagged its way between and around inmates who were now all seated on the walkway with their hands clasped behind their heads. They were about fifty yards away. Of the thirteen hundred inmates here, there had to be at least two-thirds of the population on the walkway during this movement, or approximately eight hundred men in green. There were guards everywhere in gray. They were the only thing moving and they used this as an opportunity to *kick ass*, as they termed it. It was better known among inmates as a *beatdown*. As I watched, it almost brought tears to my eyes to see these officers time and again break from the sidelines and trample innocent inmates while on their way to *beatdown* with riot batons any inmate who took a hand off of his head for whatever reason. They would do this even if they looked around or shifted their body to get better circulation through their now tiring limbs. While watching this scene, helpless to do anything about it, the thought occurred to me that although life is precious, it's strange how one can take a life under certain conditions and feel no remorse for its loss; then in the next instance feel utter compassion for a people oppressed. Total frustration overwhelmed me now as I stood there with clenched fists. I was staring through squinted eyes with tightened jaws, and I wanted to explode into rebellion and actually felt the urge if necessary to kill again if it would make them stop. You could hear the blows to the inmate's bodies, mimicking the sound of one beating a rug, and every now and then a loud crack when an inmate failed to cover up well enough to protect his head.

"And they call us savages," said Mitch in a low voice.

"Yeah Devine, I hope you make it to that minimum, man. This place ain't for the living."

I closed my eyes and sighed a deep sigh. Upon opening them, I noticed Devine had tears running down his face as he stood there in front of Tony and Mel who were now on their feet also. Diamond was just coming out of the tower at its base level.

"Just open the fucking gate, asshole!" he shouted as he slammed the door closed behind him. He was talking to a co-worker in the base level of the tower.

"What's wrong with him?" Mel asked in a low voice.

"They give him a hard time 'cause he works with us," I said.

"Yeah, but he's a cop," said Mel.

"Yeah, but he ain't a racist," I replied.

"Poor guy," said Mel and chuckled.

Suddenly, a siren blast came from behind us. It was the ambulance I had noticed coming down the hill moments earlier. It was stopped with flashers flashing and lights blinking behind us on the other side of the inside gate. They were leaving the compound also.

"Crack the gate!" Diamond shouted toward the intercom as he wheeled around directing the order to the officer whom he referred to as the asshole inside. He was impatient and obviously mad as hell. "You got an ambulance coming through. Let me out of here," he said.

The big gate's bolts freed it from its locks and as it rolled sideways allowing access to the free world, a feeling of relief came over me. I knew now no one had witnessed my involvement on the hill. *No cops anyway*, I thought. As Diamond made a U-turn in the trap, everyone but Mel started walking through the outside gate. He was a *new jack* and didn't understand the routine.

"Where's everybody going?" The van's over here, he exclaimed.

"Come on, out here," I said, "We can't board the van in there."

Mel had a puzzled look on his face and stated, "Man you guys got some strange rules."

"Jail man, we in jail. Don't try to figure these morons out, you'll drive yourself crazy," said Tony, and we lined up outside the gate awaiting Diamond to pull out of the trap, alongside us so we could board the van. As Diamond pulled up, the big gate started to close.

"What about the ambulance?" Mel asked.

"Only one vehicle at a time," I replied.

"Damn, even in an emergency?" Mel asked.

"They don't give a fuck, these motha fuckas don't care. We just a number to them," said Devine.

Now the first gate opened, and the ambulance entered the trap. It stopped briefly to be checked and logged by the tower guard who Diamond referred to as the asshole. Everyone but me was curious as to who it was inside, including Diamond. We boarded the van and waited parked at the side of the gate so as to gawk and rubberneck as it drove by. Now the second gate opened, and the ambulance pulled out of the trap and when it passed by, Diamond pulled out behind it. I looked through the van's windshield as it passed and then through the rear widows of the ambulance while Diamond tailgated it. I was surprised to see Latiff inside. I thought it would be the dead man. He was sitting up and still had on his bloodstained *kufi*. He seemed to be in agonizing pain and was reeling back and forth as he sat.

"Which one of your brothers is that?" Diamond asked.

"Never seen 'em before," I replied.

"It must be serious if they're taking him to the outside hospital," Diamond said.

"Yeah, must be," I said.

Inside the van were two bench type seats facing each other and as we sat with our backs against the walls, I noticed sitting across from me was Mitch. He had both arms folded with his legs crossed and was shaking his right foot nervously. He was looking down towards the floor with a look of total disgust on his face and it dawned on me, he was shamed by the actions he had just witnessed of white men, who were of the same race as he.

This jail had ninety-three percent of its population consisting of races other than white. It was common knowledge, among everyone there, that racism was prevalent among officers and staff, and Blacks and Hispanics were brutalized on a regular basis. Now watching the figures on the walkway getting smaller and smaller as we pulled farther away from the jail, I realized this was a day in my life that I'd never forget. Not since the war in Vietnam had I taken a life. In God's eyes it was gravely sinful to spill blood and I concluded like I had in the past that it was a justifiable death I was responsible for, and that Allah is *Rahim* (All merciful). I also realized that there were humans I had to answer to, and now that I've shed blood, the blood of a Latin King more than likely, their leaders would want revenge and would attempt to take as many Muslim lives as necessary to get it. The only people I had to answer to was the Muslim community, and as far as we were concerned, Muslim blood, or Abdul Latiffs' blood, was sacred. In jail, as a general rule, all Muslims will fight till their death if Muslim blood is spilled. Besides, if in fact the dead man and his partner were Kings they transgressed first, and Muslims are notorious for going all out in battle — the Kings knew this. As the ambulance veered off the jail's perimeter road and onto the road to town where the hospital was, we continued along the perimeter road for approximately a quarter mile to the facility's water tower.

A water tank one hundred feet tall and sixty-five feet in diameter, only the very top of the tank held the water—two and a half million gallons of it to be exact. The tank itself was wider than its base, and it looked somewhat like a giant carriage bolt, stood up on end. It was under this giant tank that the outside lawns and grounds crew kept all of their equipment including tractors and snow throwers. Here we cooked, ate breakfast and lunch, worked out and repaired tools and machinery. It also had a small workshop with every tool imaginable, running water and electricity, all enclosed in this giant circular room under the tank was every inmate's dream. A place to work out without waiting in line, a refrigerator full of food and the facilities to cook and eat to your hearts content. Although modest by outside standards, in jail, after living in an eight-by-six foot cubicle, having no refrigerator or cooking facilities or anything to eat at times for that matter, this was like Heaven and was the reason why the outside lawns and grounds crew was called, the *dream team* of Mohawk.

As we pulled up and stopped at the overhead rolling gate entrance, Mel asked, "What's up?"

"We're here," I said.

"I never realized you can get inside this place. From the jail, it just looks like a giant mushroom, but I never imagined you'd be able to get inside," he said.

Diamond got out of the van to unlock and raise the gate. All at once, I was bombarded with questions from the crew pertaining to the hit on the walkway. All inmates, not just the Kings, knew of the penalty for shedding Muslim blood. Diamond had the gate raised and was heading back to the van.

"Shit is on!" said Devine. As Diamond opened the door everyone went silent.

Rule number two in jail: *Never let the cops know what you're thinking.*

After Diamond pulled inside, "OK, who's cooking?" asked Tony.

"Not you man," he said to Devine, "We don't want scrambled pancakes like we had yesterday."

"Oh, stop crying," said Mitch, "you didn't complain until after they were all gone."

"Yeah, I saw you lickin' the plate and shit," said Devine, laughingly.

"Oh shit, you saw that?" said Tony. "I wasn't lickin' the plate, I was drinking the syrup," he said while smiling.

"Yeah, with your tongue?" said Devine.

As Diamond shut the van's engine off, "Let me cook," he said.

"Oh no!" said Mitch loudly, "I'm hungry this morning,

we ain't throwing away no food today. Devine, do your thing man, it's on you."

And that seemed to settle that. The camaraderie showed and although our little crew was multiracial and Officer Diamond was a cop, we all got along together quite well, and as far as being a team was concerned, I had never worked with Mel, but if given a tough task to do that demanded coordination, reflex and ingenuity, or the type of men you would want around in a life-or-death situation, Tony, Mitch and Devine would be my first choice. They were what you would consider to be men amongst men.

The morning passed by quickly and by lunchtime Mel was instructed on how to operate one of the small John Deer driving mowers. He had already cut most of the sprawling lawn that surrounded the water tower... As I was coming in for lunch while driving one of the Ford tractors, I pulled up alongside Diamond who was in the van parked at the edge of the road just before it intersected with the water tower's driveway. He was parked there so he could have all of us in view. After all, his job was to watch us. I had been cutting grass on either sides of the roadway and according to my watch, *chow* time was five minutes overdue.

"Are we eating today or did the governor come up with some new laws on slave labor?" I said facetiously.

He quickly looked at his watch, "Oh shit! I'm sorry, I was doing the crossword. How are you on gas?" he asked.

"I'm Ok," I said, "but the small Deere mowers should be empty soon."

"The new guy, he looks alright, how's he doing?" I asked.

"So far, so good," he replied. "This guy's *MO* (mental observation) so I can't let him get outta' my sight."

"What's he doing outside?" I asked, referring to him having outside clearance.

"I don't know, heard something about him being one of Lieutenant Nealy's special cases."

"Lieutenant Nealy, what's he got to do with it?" I asked.

"He runs the medical building now, and he's in charge of special programs for the mental observation ward. I guess he thinks this guy needs a vacation, so he stuck him out here with us. Only problem is, I gotta babysit this guy and can't get a chance to read the paper."

"Don't worry, he'll be alright, I know this guy. He used to bunk next to me."

"Oh good," said Diamond cause sometime next week we gotta' do trees."

"Trees!" I exclaimed. "What do you mean trees?" I asked, not sure of exactly what he meant by doing trees.

It had a double meaning and Diamond was an avid marijuana smoker. Quiet as it was kept, he was very discrete about this, but I had overheard him refer to his plants, as he termed them, once in the past while talking to a fellow officer. Mel, on the other hand was an addict with a major problem and didn't need any more substances in his body to fuel the fire that had already prompted his suicide attempt.

"That storm we had the other night knocked down some trees on Deputy Lape's property. You can keep an eye on this guy while I read my paper. Plus, I don't like being around those fucking chain saws with you guys," he said.

"OK, what's our cut? I hope he don't plan on paying us off with tomatoes from his garden."

"No, they're not even ripe yet. Don't worry, he'll take care of you guys," he promised.

"Yeah right! Like when we painted that captain's porch last year. All the Pepsi and potato chips we could eat and drink? One two-liter bottle of Pepsi and a big bag of chips for four guys," I replied, incredulously.

As Diamond sat slouched behind the wheel and feeling guilty for not cutting us a better deal in that instance, he said, "Yeah, that was foul. I'll make sure you guys have a party this time. Come on, let's eat," he said while cranking the engine. "I'll meet you inside. I'm gonna round up the other guys," he added, then put the van in gear and pulled off.

The land beyond the razor-wired, double-fencing that surrounded Mohawk was predominantly state-owned. Old but beautiful, large porched houses with substantial acreage were owned and maintained by the state. These houses were reserved for private use as living quarters for the top brass employees of Mohawk along with their families year-round. It was not uncommon for Diamond to take on small jobs such as the painting of the captain's porch when it wasn't that it needed painting as much as the captain wanted to change its color. Although we were employees of the state, it was common knowledge among the facility's staff and family that we the inmates worked for legal slave wages, averaging around eighteen cents per hour for thirty hours a week, or roughly eleven dollars every two weeks for sixty hours work. They also understood that we could never get rich from those wages, or even survive as a bum in the street for that matter, at that rate. They knew in order to get a decent day's work from an underpaid inmate, they had to pay an incentive fee in the form of food, none of which could be taken back inside the gate.

As I drove up the short roadway leading to the tower, I blew the horn to get Mel's attention, who was in the field still cutting the grass that surrounded it. When he looked up, I gave him the universal hand signal for assembly which is winding a straight arm in the air in a circular motion with the palm facing forward. Instantly he veered off his course from cutting grass and turned the Deere. mower in my direction. I was genuinely surprised to see him respond to it. Most military men seem to forget these time-saving hand signals once their tour of duty is over. It wasn't often I had the opportunity to use this silent but effective way of communication, so realizing the Deere still had yet more throttle, I held my fist up again and pumped my arm up and down, like tooting a train whistle. The mower instantly reached top speed. It was the signal for hurry up, and Mel understood.

When he reached alongside my tractor, "What's the matter?" Mel exclaimed.

"*Chow,*" I responded. "Infantry?" I asked.

"Boy Scouts!" he said proudly.

"You too?" I responded.

"Yep, Cub Scouts Pack 54, Boy Scouts Troop 705, Explorer Post 771," he said proudly again and smiled.

Then jokingly, I gave him the scout three fingered salute and he saluted back. After we both laughed it off, we parked the machinery in front of the tower's entrance and went inside to wash up and await the rest of the crew.

"How you feelin'?" I asked Mel while we washed our hands side by side at the slop sink.

"Better lately, a lot better now with this new job. You know, *akh*, that morning after you left for *chow*, I felt so useless to my children and family and like I was fucking up everybody's life around me. I just wanted to end it all."

"Yeah, drugs is all that," I said, "I assume you've had a change of heart?"

"It's getting better, I'm getting better and takin' it one day at a time," he said.

"You scared the hell out of me that morning," I said. "Don't be pullin' no dumb stuff like that out here, Diamond may bury you where he finds you," I said jokingly.

"So, how'd you get outside clearance?" I asked.

"You know that lieutenant, the one who came in and tore up the ticket that morning?" he said.

"Yeah, Lieutenant Nealy?" I asked.

"Well, he's in charge of programs over where I'm at," he said.

"The psych wanted to know who I associated with in this jail, along with how many times a day I shit," he added jokingly. "I told him, nobody. Then he asked me how I got along with the guys in my dorm and your name popped up. So, when I was interviewed by Lieutenant Nealy for program eligibility, your name was in my folder, and he remembered you. He punched your name into the computer, then asked me, 'How would I like to work with you outside?' I think being short to the board had a lot to do with it too."

"That's great man, so how do you like it out here?" I asked.

"This shit's nice, you can breathe out here," he said. "I ain't drove in eight years."

"Well, we'll be cutting grass all summer and you'll be tired of it after a couple of weeks," I said. "When do you go to the board?" I asked.

"Next week," he said, "or at least I was supposed to, before." At that point Mel paused then continued, "Before I fucked up," he said, in a somber voice.

"Well, look at the bright side," I said, "you still got two months after the board to show them you're alright. And they'll probably want you outta here anyway, to let parole be responsible for you," I said.

"Sounds good *akh*, but I don't know," he said. "There's some guys in my dorm, I mean my ward, who are two years past their *CR* (conditional release date), and they're still being held for observation."

"Did they do what you did?" I asked, referring to his suicide attempt.

"No, these guys are just fuckin' crazy," he said, "Thorazine zombies, they got 'em not knowing whether they're comin' or goin'," he said while shaking his head.

Just then Diamond pulled up and you could hear the sound of the mowers' engines of the other tractors driven by Devine, Tony and Mitch coming closer and closer as they raced back in response to their late *chow call*.

"I'm cooking!" Diamond shouted as he ran inside and raced to the refrigerator.

"Wash your hands," I said out loud.

"What's up with this guy wanting to cook all the time?" said Mel.

"From what I understand he does the same thing at home, but his wife be getting on him about messin' up all the groceries, so he be tryin' to practice on us," I said.

"Oh, this dude's bugged," said Mel as he shook the water from his hands.

After Mel dried his hands with a paper towel, he unfolded it and neatly spread it open on the drain board, then lowered his head so his face was directly over it. He then proceeded to remove his contact lenses, that up till now, I had no idea he wore.

"Dammit! Motha fucka!" he exclaimed.

"Don't move *akh* please, I dropped a lens," he said.

As Diamond approached us at the sink, he paused momentarily and watched Mel as he was looking for his lens while on his knees.

"Oh, you guys smoking crack? Don't pick up any *UFOs*," he said jokingly.

Both Mel and I looked at him in astonishment and then looked at each other without saying a word until Diamond took another step toward the sink.

"Hold Up!" I said. "He dropped a contact lens."

"Got it," said Mel, "I'll wear my glasses tomorrow," he said.

"I'm doing the cooking," said Diamond loudly to the rest of the crew as they filed in.

As Mel and I moved away from the now crowded sink, Mel stated to me, "A crack-smokin' cop."

"Well, I'll be…" I said and we both shook our heads in

disappointment, more so in remorse for not just Diamond, but for anyone who fell into that trap.

In the seedy, low life environments of the crack houses in New York City's ghettos, the term *UFO*, when associated with crack, meant something some users would pick up or find, other than crack, while desperately searching the floor or anywhere else they saw anything that resembled it. It was not a term one used or knew unless they had been there. Diamond was living a double life. Both Mel and I realized that if Diamond continued down that road, that it was just a matter of time before his crack habit would eventually get the best of him, as it did everyone who indulged in this criminally wasteful pastime. At best he would become a functional addict and continue to maintain his work habits or keep a job in other words, but nothing more than just that. The typical lifestyle of a functional addict was to work to get high, never having enough drugs and always crying broke.

"Well, you can't fuck up hamburgers," said Tony as he approached the picnic table with a plate of four triple decker cheeseburgers.

"Diamond can," said Devine.

The temperature had reached the low eighties and we carried one of three picnic tables outside the tower and placed it in the sunlight so as to take advantage of the nice weather.

"It's chow?" asked Mitch.

"Yeah," said Tony, "I stood over him and made sure he didn't burn 'em up."

"Did you leave us any?" I asked jokingly.

"Oh yeah Bilal, you know it," he said. "I made fifteen

doubles for you guys and Diamond's still flippin' more. You guys tell him when to stop, I'll be busy eating," he said.

"Damn, you guys eat like that?" said Mel.

"Every day," said Mitch. "Don't spread it around the jail," he said, "or they'll probably cut back on our rations."

After eating, the six of us including Diamond, laid outstretched on the grass enjoying the sunshine. My thoughts drifted back to earlier this morning and the sequence of events that had taken place on the inside. No one had mentioned anything about it all day, but like Devine had said this morning before we got out the van, it's on. I didn't know exactly what to expect but I did know all hell was about to break loose. And I had to somehow notify the Muslim's *shirta* squad (Muslim security) of exactly what had taken place and all I knew of the incident.

After lunch, we all returned to our assigned areas and completed the day as usual. We continued to cut grass until Diamond rounded us up for the facility *go back* (when all programs ended and all inmates returned to their respective dorm areas). After being searched and leaving the trap, now back on the inside, as we walked along the east gate walkway, I could see a dark area on the asphalt up the hill. It was the spot where the dead man lay earlier this morning. As I looked toward my left, approaching the fork in the walkway, I noticed a number of smaller spots of the same shade as the larger one up the hill. To my left was the programs building, it was to where the inmates who were beat down this morning were on their way before they encountered the baton-wielding guards in gray. These smaller spots on the asphalt marked the locations where inmates were horribly brutalized. They were the dried unwashed blood stains, such as the larger one up the hill left by the dead man.

Now the inmates in the program building poured out of the doorway for the *go back*. We, the outside crew, were always given a head start of sixty seconds before the rest of the facility, another fringe benefit of the dream team. It was for security purposes, to not have the gate in operation anytime during a movement. Such as it was, it did put us at the front of the movement.

"Damn, you think these fuckin' animals would wash this shit away," said Mitch in a disgusted tone of voice, referring to the large blood stain which we now encountered.

It was a morbid sight of undoubtedly a violent death scene. There was unquestionably a considerable amount more blood than it was when I turned and looked back this morning. Literally thousands of flies of the shiny, iridescent, greenish species covered the area entirely, and formed swarming clusters on the darker areas where thick clots of blood stopped in its flow.

"They trying to stir up some shit," said Devine, referring to the administrations staff, "These motha fuckas gonna get mad when they see this shit."

And oh, how right he was. It was a tactic used by the facility when they needed more information. Their reasoning was to provoke an incident to capture more suspects, as to shake the needle out of the haystack. Evidently, they didn't have a suspect other than Latiff. With him having been wounded in the manner in which he was, and there not being a murder weapon, the cops knew that there had to be someone else involved. Someone they didn't have.

There was no stopping on the walkway. So as we passed the blood stain, not in any particular hurry, we slowed our pace and shortened our steps, subsequently allowing ourselves to be overcome and engulfed by the forgoing inmates. Now well past the gruesome scene, we heard squeamish remarks coming from behind. Moments later, my name was called by one of these voices who was now only a few feet behind me. It was Mighty Mouse, a six-foot-six-inch, two-hundred-and-seventy-pound, power-lifting homosexual who had won the first-place award in competition for three years in a row.

Mousey, as his companions affectionately called him, acquired his name by wearing his hair drawn straight back into two bleached orange puffs of hair resembling mouse ears. He was a blazingly blatant and flamboyant, giant of a homosexual who spoke in a very articulate and feminine dialect; a booty bandit rapist who cliqued with several other sexual predators who had the same MO (modus operandi).

"Hi Bilal," he said again, in an irritating, artificially feminine tone of voice.

I heard him the first time he called but chose to ignore him.

As he walked alongside me and a half step behind, "How do you know my name?" I asked indignantly.

"Everyone knows who you are, "he said, "I just thought there was something you should know."

"Yeah, and what's that?" I responded.

"I sold some bullets to one of my girlfriend's boyfriend this morning, and he's a King," he said.

"Bullets?" I interrupted.

"Yes, some .22 bullets I smuggled in a long time ago, you know, for a zip gun. If I had my operation, I could have hidden the whole damn gun," he said and smirked.

"Yeah, so what's up?" I asked.

"Well, the word is out that you had something to do with that thing on the walkway this morning," he said. "Before I even knew why he wanted them, I had already sold them to him. I'm sorry," he said, "I used to be a Muslim, but I just wasn't ready to leave my old man. I still believe in Allah, and I don't want to see any Muslims get hurt."

"Who's your girlfriend's boyfriend?" I asked.

"One of the King's hit men," he said. "I can't give you any names, but just watch your back."

"Thanks," I replied, as he dropped back with his friends.

"What's up with that?" said Mel, who had the same puzzled look on his face, as did the rest of the crew: Mitch, Tony and Devine.

"He had a message for me," I said.

"Oh, for a minute there…" said Mitch and laughed.

"Don't even go there," I said, threateningly with a smile.

As we rounded the next turn in the walkway, the entrance pathway leading to the medical building was only a few yards away.

"Okay, I'll see ya'll tomorrow," said Mel and quickly turned and hurriedly walked up the path.

"Tell Nealy I said hi," I said loudly.

And without breaking stride or looking back, he raised his right fist in acknowledgement.

"Where's he going?" said Devine.

"You ask too many questions D," said Tony.

"This guy's *MO* ward?" asked Mitch.

I shrugged my shoulders while cocking my head to one side without saying a word, and with that everyone seemed to have gotten the message. Sometimes silence speaks louder than words…

By now we were well behind the inmates at the front of the movement. Knowing the word was out that I had some connection with this morning's incident, I decided to get indoors or back to my dorm as quickly as possible. I focused on my surroundings and noticed a group of approximately ten Hispanic men walking about thirty feet in front of us. Three of which were glancing over their shoulders and looking back directly at me. I had seen this setup many times before, at this and every other jail I had the displeasure of being a resident. It was a hit squad, and unlike my previous experiences, I was the subject. I now checked behind me and to my surprise, were at least fifty Muslims walking abreast and filled the walkway from curb to curb, They were in three ranks only ten feet behind, all donning *kufis* and holding back the movement so as to not let anyone pass.

"We see 'em *akh*," said Big Brother Malik (Ma-leek) as we fondly referred to him.

He was *wahzier* of *shirta* (head of security) and just his presence alone was enough to make anyone he accompanied feel secure. He was truly a massive and physically powerful man who stood six-feet-five inches and weighed almost two-hundred-and-sixty-pounds. I hadn't even realized it but there was no one between the Muslims and the small group of Kings, but my crew and myself for the last few moments.

Suddenly, "*Takbir!*" was yelled by Big Brother, and a thunderous response of, "A*llahu Akbar* (God is the greatest!)!" in unison was chorused by my Muslim brothers and myself (when a Muslim says *Takbir* – pronounced takbeer – every Muslim in earshot responds with *Allahu Akbar*).

"Bilal, what's going on?" asked Mitch very concernedly.

"It's okay," I assured my coworkers and watched the small band of Kings high tail it into the crowd in front of them.

"I'll see you guys in the morning, I gotta go," I said to my crew mates.

"Shit is on," said Devine and grinned devilishly. "Can I hang?" he asked.

"You know what you gotta do," I said, referring to him coming into the fold of *Al Islam* and restructuring his belief in Allah.

As it stood, he was a Black Muslim who incorporated Black nationalism into Islam, and it was a major difference of belief between he and I and the fifty odd Muslims who had just *Takbired* with impressive results. Devine and I had also spoken on this subject many times in the past. We had both agreed that although we both believed in Allah, it was not as simple as the enemy of my enemy is my brother.

I had forgotten my *kufi* on the drain board back at

the water tower and anticipated a scolding from Alim as soon as I approached the group, but to my surprise he was nowhere present. I deliberately slowed down to allow myself to fall back into the front rank, next to Big Brother Malik.

"*Assalamu alaikum*, my brothers. *Shukran* (thanks)," l said loudly.

"*Walaikum salaam* and *afwan* (you're welcome)," was many the response.

"Myyy Brother Bilal," said Malik as he rested a heavy arm across my shoulders.

"You OK?" he asked.

"Yeah, I'm alright," I said. "They took that new brother, Abdul Latiff, to the outside hospital this morning," I said.

"Yeah, we know, he's back at the infirmary," he said.

"He's back! How is he?" I asked.

"They stitched him up, gave him a transfusion, and brought him back," he said.

"You know that kid died," he said.

"Yeah, I know," I said in a somber voice.

"Don't worry," said Big Brother as he pulled me closer to his side in a comforting manner, then said, "Allah wouldn't put nothin' on you that you couldn't handle. You got steel?" he asked, referring to a weapon.

"No," I replied.

"You gonna need some," he said.

"It's on now, and these guys ain't playing," he said.

"Big Brother," I said, "these guys got guns?"

"Guns?" he replied. "What makes you say that?" he said.

"That homo Mighty Mouse back there told me he sold

a King some bullets for zip guns this morning. They should have a few made by now. All it takes is a radio antenna, a block of wood, some rubber bands and a cabinet latch that anybody can steal from the carpentry shop," I stated convincingly.

"Now we got problems," he said, "but we also got a secret weapon."

"What's that?" I asked.

"We have Allah on our side," he said and smiled.

"Let 'em through!" he commanded, referring to the inmates behind us, as he strode at a steady pace never turning his head, only tilting it forward to look over his shades every now and then. He carried with him even when alone, which was rare, an air of invincibility that no man in his right mind would dare challenge without having second thoughts.

As I greeted and made small talk with my Muslim brothers, the inmates who were backed up behind the Muslim ranks trickled slowly, and with a somewhat cautious curiosity, passed the now more relaxed Muslims. They seemed to gawk in reverence at us. It was common knowledge that Muslims were a formidable, organized force to be reckoned with if crossed. These *kufi*-clad men of peace had just displayed a *Takbir* in public, which could be startling to anyone who has never experienced or witnessed it done by a large group of Muslim men. It can get your undivided attention instantly, to say the least.

"Mouse!" I heard Brother Malik say loudly.

I looked up to see Mighty Mouse while passing, abruptly respond to Big Brother's call and point to himself.

"Come here!" ordered Malik. As Mighty Mouse

walked up beside him, "You look ridiculous. Don't get too close to me," said Big Brother. He continued with, "I'm gonna ask you this one time," he said, "What's his name? And where's he lock?"

"Miguel is his name, Miguel. He's in the honor dorm, they call him Loco," he said.

"Thanks. Get outta here, and you need to do something with that damn hair," he said.

Mighty Mouse quickly walked away and caught up with his friends.

"Brother Bilal!" he called.

"Yeah," I answered and approached him alongside.

"You know of a Loco in the honor dorm?" he asked.

"No," I said.

"Well, that's the guy with the bullets," he said.

"There were two guys, right?" he asked.

"Right," I said.

"Well, I hope Loco is the guy we want. He spilled Muslim blood and he's gonna pay," he said, "and all the zip guns in the world, ain't gonna stop us from giving him his just due. The axe is being sharpened right now while we're talking."

As I pondered the thought, "Big Brother," I said.

"Yeah?" he replied.

I paused momentarily, "Never mind," I said, and we continued to walk in silence.

Malik was still looking straight ahead with an air of dignity and pride, and every so often tucking his chin to momentarily look over his shades at things one in a position of security may find interesting.

Suddenly, "*Allahu Akbar*, on point," he commanded over his right shoulder.

Most of the Muslims were behind us and still very aware of their surroundings, but Big Brother Malik had towering height in comparison to the average man, so he saw what we saw not. I strained to see what the alert was in reference to. The crowd in front of us was parting from the center and through the middle of the movement there appeared sporadically, approximately thirty officers in full riot gear, now forming a blockade.

"Easy," was the order commanded by Big Brother, "I don't want no heroes."

Now the same feeling of hopelessness came over me. The same sinking of my heart to my stomach that I felt at the east gate this morning when Officer Diamond asked, *Who was the last one up the walkway?* Unconsciously, I slowed my pace until I was a full step back.

"Don't stop, *akhi*," said Malik." Don't show these *kafirs* no fear," he said.

And I quickly took my place alongside him. I looked behind me to see only Muslims still walking. The rest of the inmates had stopped and were in a state of semi panic, some fifty feet behind. Then through the center of the blockade, from behind the wall of riot shields, appeared a white-shirted sergeant wearing a helmet with a face shield and a holstered baton at his side. He stepped in front of the blockade then folded his arms and awaited our approach.

Finally, "Who's the leader here?" he asked, and the suspense was over.

As we came to a stop, the entire group took positions opposite the police in two ranks that spread beyond the curbs and onto the grass only fifteen feet away. They then folded their arms as if in defiance of the clear and present danger.

"Who's the leader here?" he asked again.

"Allah is our leader," said Big Brother Malik. "Is there a problem?" he asked.

"There will be if I don't get any answers," said the officer. "Why are all of you wearing your *kufis*? Are you at war with the Kings?" he asked.

"We are men of peace," said Malik, "and we don't want any trouble with them or you."

"Why are you all together?" asked the sergeant.

"After what happened this morning, we're just keeping an eye on each other," said Malik.

"Well, the guy who got killed was a King, and one of you guys did it," he said.

"What makes you say that?" said Malik.

"What do you think, we're stupid?" said the sergeant.

Big Brother stood silent.

"All I know is, if there's any more bloodshed on this walkway, or in the yard, or in the dorms, or anywhere in this compound all-a-your asses will be in a sling," he said, "and no more waiting for each other in front of the school building either. When that movement starts, get your asses in gear and keep it in gear. And that goes for all of yous," he said.

Then he reached for his baton, and while looking up at Big Brother slipped his hand through the leather thong and wrapped it tightly around it, gripping the baton as if ready for action. There was dead silence. He then turned and walked back and forth slapping the baton in his opposite palm, looking at each of us in the eyes as he passed.

"Which one of you tough guys is the killer?" he finally asked as he stopped directly in front of me.

He now looked at Brother Malik and said, "You, big guy, I'm sure you know."

Big Brother never dropped his eyes in acknowledgement. He was having a stare down with the shielded officers behind the blockade and the tension in the air was so thick, you could have cut it with a knife. The sergeant folded one arm across his chest and when he raised the baton unknowingly by us to rest it on his shoulder, the sudden repositioning of the Muslim ranks got his attention and he quickly lowered it to a non-threating position and stepped back.

He focused on me, then looked around at the ranks, then back at me, and said, "Where's your *kufi*?"

I didn't answer; instead, I looked him in the eyes and stood silent. I was sizing him up, ready to take action if necessary. I had decided if I was to be physically abused, I was not going down without a fight and had made up my mind that I would not stop fighting until I was in handcuffs.

"I'm talking to you, boy," he said while pointing his baton.

Now the adrenalin seemed to boil in my veins, and as he attempted to repeat the order, he nudged me with the baton, high on my left shoulder. In a circular motion, I swept my left arm over the baton and tucked it under my arm pit while grabbing hold of it near his hand. The leather thong was still wrapped around his hand, and he froze with a look of shock in his eyes. I slowly started rotating the baton in the opposite direction, still staring him in the eyes until the pain from twisting his arm started to show, then I instantly released the baton and him without inflicting any real pain, just enough to let him know that he could have been had. His back up didn't make a move. They were outnumbered almost two to one.

The legacy of the Attica Riots (Attica Prison Massacre) in Attica, New York on September 9th,1971, lasted four days. Lead by The Nation of Islam (the Black Muslims), it bequest upon all Muslims in jail till today, an unerring reputation for being treated with decency and respect by inmates and guards alike. And any *kafir* cop who was foolish enough to unreasonably brutalize a Muslim would be hard pressed to find another cop to help him, mainly from fear of retaliation.

"Did you see that. Did you see that?" he repeated. "He tried to break my fucking arm," he said while looking for support from his co-workers.

Then his walkie-talkie received a transmission, "Come in Seven-one-eight, come in now!"

And the sergeant responded. He was seven-one-eight. "This is Seven-one-eight over," he said.

"This is Nealy in the medical building," and the sergeant looked up at the third-floor window to see Lieutenant Nealy watching everything from his office. "We don't need a riot on our hands. Do it by the book when it comes to them, I'm out," he said.

As the sergeant holstered his walkie-talkie, he stared at me with a look of vengeance. *If looks could kill,* I thought. Now frustrated and thoroughly embarrassed, he turned towards his men and waved his arms with the baton in hand implying, *it's over, let's go back*, and without another word, the blockade of officers disassembled their wall of shields and returned from whence they came. As the guards left the scene, we stood our ground momentarily, undirected and without orders to continue the movement. Then from behind us came whistles and cheers from the inmates who had stopped and separated themselves from the Muslims. They were impressed and glad to see the guards intimidated and finally getting the short end of the stick for a change. No pun intended.

"Myyy Brother Bilal," said Big Brother as he laid a heavy arm across my shoulders once again. "You gotta' show me that move when you get time" he said, in jest. "How'd you do it?" he asked, and contorted his free arm to imitate me in the manner in which I subdued the sergeant.

We all had a very good laugh, and it thoroughly broke the tension we all had been subjected to. But our troubles were by no means over, in fact they were just beginning. The Kings wanted blood in retaliation for a botched hit gone bad. We wanted the man responsible for spilling Muslim blood and like Big Brother Malik said, All the guns in the world wouldn't stop us. The police on the other hand were a constant enemy. We knew their habits and how they moved; besides, they were more of an obstacle than a deterrent. I now needed an equalizer. I was the prime target of the King hit squad and felt the next time I encountered them I might not be so lucky. Abdul Latiff was housed in the medical building which was maximum security. He and I now were on the King hit list but with him under twenty-four-hour guard, it was just a matter of time that I again would be the subject of another King *TOS* attempt.

As we continued the movement, we could see the guards forcibly pushing their way past the inmates, who incidentally had stopped to turn around and watch the confrontation. We heard jeers and shouts of, *boo*, coming from the inmates as the guards made their way through the crowd headed towards the mess hall. These inmates had encountered these same guards as they shoved and pushed their way through the middle of the movement, on their way to confront us. Now as they returned unsuccessful in their mission to interrogate us through means of public intimidation, they had to suffer the pangs of a public humiliation by inmates who scrutinized their every move.

"Them niggas is maaad," I heard one inmate say, laughingly referring to the guards as he passed me by.

As I took a candid look around observing this group of dedicated and devout Muslims, I thought, *how nice it was to see a group of men proclaiming their religious beliefs in public by all donning kufis.* Ironically, it wasn't often even in the free world outside the gate that I had the opportunity to be surrounded by so many do-gooders at one time like I was now. I then criticized myself at that moment. I should have known better, I thought, I shouldn't even be here in jail. I was an indoctrinated Muslim before coming to prison and most of these men didn't find God until after they were incarcerated. I felt shamed, to think that these men were ready to risk their lives and possibly lose them over me because in their hearts, they felt it was sanctioned by God. In my mind I felt I didn't deserve it.

This was my penance, my punishment, my wakeup call. *How great was the struggle, within the forgiveness of sins*, I thought. We all make mistakes, and this is a learning experience that I'll never forget. Besides they're all here protecting me as I protected Abdul Latiff. I shuddered to think of where Latiff would be right now if I wasn't there this morning. Then I shuddered again to think, that I was. *Allah is the best of planners*, I concluded.

Most of these men became epiphanized at a very low time in their lives and questioned the quality of their existence. When they realized there was no other way to go but up, they reached for the long hand of God. They needed to be helped out of the hole in life that they themselves had dug and found themselves imprisoned in. I could argue that the measure of a man's life is gauged by the amount of positive influence he has on his fellow man. When one has a positive influence on the masses, such as Malcolm X for instance, to do the right thing, I'd say, therein lies the greatness of man. His eloquent discourse and orations, and his unwavering courage in the face of opposition cost him his life. He paid with the ultimate sacrifice while trying to bring God's word, and justice and equality to the masses. Was it worth it?...

The measure of a man's soul can only be determined by God, so it would be presumptuous and ignorant of me to say. I can say, that even in his absence here on earth, it's reinforcing for me to know that a man as great as he, had the same basic morals and religious beliefs as I, and in a sense, he lost his life while trying to save the souls of others. Malcom was assassinated three blocks away from my childhood home. I was a teenager in the crowd at the side door when they removed his body from the Audubon Ballroom in Washington Heights, upper Harlem in NYC. As a teenager, I used to hear him speak on a wooden stage erected outside, near the Apollo Theater in Harlem, when he was a follower of Elijah Muhammad. Although posthumously, I feel spiritually connected to him as this was, in a sense, a brush with greatness for me.

As we approached the mess hall, we found that the guards had aligned themselves outside against the brick wall, standing abreast at ease, in a casual stance. Their shields held loosely with one arm and their batons all gripped tightly in the other hand. It was a lame display of authority.

"Aw man, what is this, a scare tactic?" said Big Brother Malik in a low voice then shook his head while smiling.

I smiled too, until someone in the crowd, who had already passed the mess hall, yelled, "Oh shit! It's the march of the wooden soldiers."

There was always a comedian in the crowd. It wasn't often but sometimes someone would seize the opportunity and verbally humiliate the guards if they thought they could get away with it. The whole movement went up in a roar of laughter. It was so funny, that the guards started laughing themselves, except for one, Sergeant Seven-one-eight. He stood there apart from the other officers, one hand resting on his holstered baton and his helmet in the other propped against his upper thigh, staring, looking directly at me as I passed. I thought it best not to make eye contact with him. I felt I needn't give him anything else to remember me by. As it was, I had the last word in our battle of wits back on the walkway. I remember thinking, I don't like the way he's looking at me, and hoping he would cause me no problems in the future.

We were coming upon the fork in the walkway where a path led across the huge, manicured lawn to the four smaller dorms across from building twenty-two.

"*Allahu Akbar!*" shouted Big Brother, he was now some ten yards in front of me. All of the Muslims looked in his direction. "East yard, on the *PM rec movement*, tell everybody!" he shouted. "Bilal," he called, looking in my direction, "Read *Surah: 5, Ayat: 33*," he said, then gestured like Latiff had done that morning and held up his fist facing it toward me with his index finger pointing upwards, implying, there is but one God.

He then turned and walked up the path leading to the four smaller dorms across the way. Read *Surah: 5, Ayat: 33*? I said to myself. Was he serious about the axe being sharpened while we spoke? I pondered again...

"Bilal!" shouted Alim from behind. I turned to see Alim making his way through the crowd towards me. When he reached, "Here man, take this," he said.

He was slightly out of breath from trying to catch up with us. "I had a hard time gettin' it past the guards in the school building," he said and slipped me a hefty, handy, shiny piece of flat steel.

"What's this?" I asked.

"Check it out, when you get home," he said. "It's a new idea I have for pocketknives."

"This thing is a knife?" I asked, while discretely slipping it into my pants pocket."

"Yeah, but don't press the button till you wanna use it."

"Button?" I questioned. "Man, you crazy," I said laughingly. "What is it, a switch blade?"

"Better," he said, "the blade pops up from inside the handle."

"What are you, a mad scientist?" I asked jokingly.

"The mad machinist," he said proudly and smiled.

"Man, you crazy," I said again, and laughed.

"What happened to you this morning? I can't leave you alone for a minute," he said jokingly while looking around with an air of caution. "From now on, don't go anywhere by yourself. Them Kings are sneaky, and they gawn be on you like colds on ice. You got Kings in your dorm?" he asked.

"I'm not sure," I said, "I haven't seen anybody throwin' signs."

Most gangs in prison have secret hand gestures and greetings that they use to beckon to one another in passing.

"Well watch your back, Bilal. I don't wanna have to catch a body up in here over you," he said and smiled.

I couldn't shake the thought of using an axe in retaliation. I figured that when it came to large weapons in Mohawk, Alim was the man behind them.

"Alim," I said while we walked toward building twenty-two, "do we have an axe?"

Alim smiled. "Do we!" he said affirmatively. "A couple of summers ago, we had a fire in the gym. A fire truck came through here during the *PM go back*, at night. It left here, minus one big, red axe. Only the *shirta* team knows where it's kept. Why'd you ask me that?" he said.

"Big Brother said something about it. He also told me to read, *5:33*," I said.

Alim raised his eyebrows and said surprisingly, "He told you that?"

"Yeah," I said. "I just hope I ain't elected to do the choppin'," I added.

"Nah man, don't worry," he said. "You have to volunteer for that kinda work. Plus, you gotta' be *shirta*," he added.

As we reached building twenty-two, a feeling of relief came over me. It was as though I reached home, real home. A feeling of safeness overwhelmed me for an instant. Then consciously keeping things in perspective, I glanced over my shoulder and entered the building with caution. I reached in my pocket and felt for the knife given to me by Alim. It was comfortable to hold. I felt for the button that he spoke of. There it was, conveniently right under my thumb. Truthfully, I was paranoid momentarily, and wondered how I was going to keep my wits about me and survive this dilemma…Watching my back was now going to be a full-time job.

"Now remember brother, don't go nowhere by yourself. Wait for me here at *chow*," said Alim.

We were in the lobby of building twenty-two. My dorm was downstairs and Alim's was up. Suddenly I noticed a group of Muslims in the stairwell. Although housed in various dorms, they were residents of *the projects* also. They were keeping out of sight of the guard who was standing at the other end of the lobby. They had secretly congregated in the stairwell ready to come to my aid if I was attacked. Of the six dorms in building twenty-two, there were over three hundred inmates. Of the three hundred inmates, many of them were Kings. It was assuring to know, that if

I were to need help in the event of an attack, it would be virtually just over my shoulder.

I entered the stairwell with Alim, and before I descended the stairs, "My brothers, good lookin' out," I said.

The stairwell was crowded with inmates hurriedly making their way to their respective dorms. I was the only Muslim going downstairs and needless to say, with my hand in my pocket. I was totally aware of any movement around me and was more than ready to defend myself if need be.

As I neared the bottom of the staircase, "Hey Bilal!" was shouted by Alim from upstairs, "Don't forget your *kufi*," he said. I decided not to respond.

As I entered my dorm, I customarily glanced at the guard desk to see who was on duty. It was always a pleasure to find someone other than officer Humphrey. He was the one who eventually decided *not* to call me dog food. It was our regular morning officer, Officer Pulaski. He was seated leaning back with the chair against the wall, his arms folded, and his feet crossed and propped up on the desk. We made eye contact briefly.

"Chillin'?" I asked as I passed.

"Chillin'," he answered with a smile.

I walked down the long isle, passing cubicles on both sides of me toward my quarters, *the penthouse*. Inmates were in some of the cubes just coming back from their programs and classes. One of these inmates saw me coming, rested his elbows atop the low partition to his cube and waited.

"Bilal, how you doin'?" he said. "What's up with the Muslims and the Kings," he inquired.

"Getting rough out there," was my only reply.

I entered the small, four cubicle room and found it quiet and a bit musty. I opened the window to the room next to my cube and sat on my bunk. I leaned and looked over the partition through the wide entryway to my quarters. No one was coming. I quickly pulled the knife from my pocket and inspected it. It looked like a short flat, rectangular piece of shiny steel. I hefted it in my right hand, then tossed it to my left, flipped it twice, then tossed it back into my right. It was of comfortable weight and just large enough to fit a man-sized hand. I looked for the button and at first, I didn't see it. I then noticed a small, thin circle at one end of a slot. It was the bottom of the button. I flipped it over, I found that it only protruded slightly. It seemed very well made. I glanced back at the doorway; it was still clear. The button sat in a small, elongated slot. I pressed it, and nothing happened. I pushed the button to the other end of the slot and still nothing happened. I pressed it, and with a sharp click, I was suddenly holding a short double-edged dagger. I was impressed. I tried to wiggle the blade; it was firmly set. I had an old newspaper in my locker. I doubled it, then laid it on the floor alongside my bunk. I laid back and quickly but firmly swung my arm down hard, stabbing the newspaper, testing the knife for durability – It passed the test. I slid the button back and pressed it; the blade retracted automatically. Once I did this, I put it back in my pocket and sat up. Alim was a tool and die maker at a well-known, high-end machine shop in Brooklyn before coming to prison. I had known this all along. I had never seen a knife quite like this and realized Alim was a true craftsman. I would never look at him in the same light again.

I could hear Woody's unmistakable laugh. A few moments later, he and Rico walked in together.

"Man, it's stuffy in here," said Woody while Rico opened the other window to our room.

"Bilal, what's happening my brother," greeted Woody.

"Nothin' much," I said.

"No?" said Rico, and the way he said it, I realized he knew more than I would have liked him to. "Nothing much?" said Rico, looking back at me smiling.

Now I was positive that he knew of my involvement on the walkway this morning. I looked away, picked up the newspaper from the floor and put it back in my locker.

Don't tell me the whole jail knows about this, I thought and laid back on my bunk, fearing the cat was out of the bag.

"What we havin' for *chow*?" asked Woody as he arranged his textbooks in his locker.

"Spaghetti," answered Rico.

"Spaghetti?" said Woody. "Damn, what's the alternative?" he asked.

"I don't know," said Rico.

"Veggie burgers," I said.

"Veggie burgers! Aww man," complained Woody.

"Yep," I said. "And cake!" I added. I didn't eat prison cake, and both Woody and Rico knew this.

It was known by my dorm mates that I was privy to the daily menu. As a member of the *dream team*, we were allowed access to the kitchen pantry before leaving the compound every morning before we left for work outside the gate. With permission to take with us any of the food items on the menu that day, we knew beforehand what items were being served for *chow*.

"Cake!" both Woody and Rico exclaimed simultaneously.

"With frosting?" asked Woody while holding onto the partition at the entrance way to my cubicle.

He was smiling down at me, with his eyes aglow at the mere mention of cake.

"Bilal, Bilal," cried Rico as he came running past Woody into my cube and sat in my chair. Rico was half-seated with one knee on the floor and his hands clasped like he was praying. "Come on Bilal, it's my turn for your cake. Woody got it last time," he said.

"He's right, Woody," I said.

"Aw man," said Woody, then conceded to it.

"Why don't y'all leave that man alone?" said Mr. Watts in his usual slow way of talking when he's not excited or aggravated. He now completed our small family-like group as he walked in at a slow pace. "Y'all always up in that man's face for something. Bilal, I don't know how you can stand it." he said, "Look at 'em, like two little beggar boys in front'a church on Sunday morning."

Mr. Watts stepped into his cube next to mine as Woody and Rico returned to theirs. He then peered over the partition that separated our cubes, looked down at me and smiled, then winked as if to say watch this. He had overheard Rico and Woody vying for my cake.

"Damn, I had this toothache all day," he said while holding his jaw.

"You eatin' your cake?" asked Woody enthusiastically.

"What cake?" said Mr. Watts.

"We got cake for *chow*," said Woody.

"Oh yeah! I ain't givin' up my cake," said Mr. Watts while shaking his head *no*.

"Now how you gawn eat cake with a toothache?" said Woody.

"Like this!" said Mr. Watts, and he reached in his mouth and pulled out both his upper and lower partial plates.

As Watts stood there, he bounced his lips up and down, and while crossing his eyes, twisted his head from side to side. It was the funniest thing I've seen an old man do, to date.

"Now how I'm gonna get a toothache and I ain't got tooth the first," he said, sounding like Gabby Hayes, an old toothless cowboy from the black and white movie era.

"Oh shit, did you see his lips?" said Woody, laughing hysterically.

Watts replaced his dentures.

"Now, you know how you can get my cake," he said. Rico laughed at Woody loudly after Watts' statement. "It'll cost ya, son. You gotta pay up, just like er'body else," he said, then swung his towel over his shoulder.

He then turned and walked out on his way to the lavatory.

"Awe c'mon Mr. Watts," said Woody as Watts walked away. "Mr. Watts! Mr. Watts!" he called again. "Damn!"

cried Woody as he walked out behind Watts to see if he could make a reasonable deal for the cake.

I hadn't forgotten that Rico knew of my involvement. From the looks of it, Woody and Mr. Watts hadn't a clue. As I lay there on my bunk with my hands clasped behind my head, I figured it best to take advantage of the privacy and find out how much Rico knew of my involvement, if any.

"Rico!" I called.

"Un momento," he said.

Moments later, he walked up to the entrance way to my cube. He rested his palms on the tops of the partition, on either side.

"You OK?" he asked, concernedly.

"Yeah man, have a seat," I said while sitting up.

"I know that guy," he said in his Puerto Rican accent. "I know him good," he added. "I know him from the weight yard, we talk all the time. I tell him, Ramon, get out of that King shit. All the time I tell him that. No, but he likey, he like to hurt people. God bless him now," said Rico, then made the sign of the cross and kissed his hand.

"Are there any Kings in this dorm?" I asked.

"Yeah," he said, "Raul in twenty-eight and Edmundo in thirty-six."

"Just two?" I asked.

"Yeah." said Rico. "But don't worry, this is Netas dorm now," he said proudly. "I'm like god in here," he boasted while slapping his chest twice, "They make trouble for you inside, I kill them. They know. They no pull that shit in my dorm. Outside it's OK, no inside. Be careful, just watch you back. You my friend, Bilal."

I smiled weakly, then said, "Thanks."

Rico stood up, "Smile," he said while reaching out for my hand.

As we shook hands, Rico pulled me up to stand. He was much shorter than I.

He held me by both arms, looked me in the eyes and said, "You kill that Doberman dog, you kill that big guy, you good man Bilal, you'll be OK. Don't worry," he assured me. "Don't worry," he repeated, then slapped my left bicep as he turned and walked back to his cubicle.

It was encouraging to know Rico and I were close enough as friends, that although I was a Muslim, it didn't matter. Being the leader of the Netas at Mohawk meant that he was a very powerful man. If he said I was safe inside, I was safe inside. Knowing this meant at least I could move around freely about the dorm and wash areas with less worry of retaliation from the Kings. It still was not a guarantee though, and because of this, I was to spend many a night sleeping, as they say, with one eye open.

"Man, stop followin' me. I done told you what it's gawn cost now!" said Mr. Watts to Woody as they made their way back into *the penthouse*.

"Like a goddamn cunt hound in heat," Watts said to himself as he hung his now damp towel over the back of the chair in his cube. "Over cake! Boy you need to be 'shamed of yourself," Watts turned and said to Woody.

"Man, the only thing I'm ashamed of is eatin' pussy!" said Woody.

"What!" exclaimed Watts. "Mean to tell me you don't eat no pussy boy?"

"Nah man," said Woody in a low voice. He didn't sound too convincing.

"You married?" asked Watts.

"Hell no!" answered Woody.

"Oh, 'cause you show me a man don't eat no pussy, I'll show you a man I can take his wife," Watts said with a look of confidence.

Woody burst into laughter.

"You?" he said, "You Mr. Watts, gawn take somebody's wife? Man, you dreamin'…"

"Boy," Watts started, "women get weak in the knees when they see me comin'. All's I gotta do is pop these teeth out. Shit, my little girlie back home calls me Gumby. The bitch gives me cauliflower ear every time she spends the night."

Woody burst into laughter again, but this time he was accompanied by Rico and me. There are no second servings in state prisons and with agreeing to give up his whole tray of food, Woody did strike a deal with Watts for his cake.

CHAPTER 5

Nominations

I met Alim and about ten other Muslims outside of building twenty-two on my way to *PM chow*. All went well without incident at the mess hall, and I returned safely to my dorm. Now lying on my bunk awaiting the recreation movement, my mind wandered. I knew we had a meeting of the minds in the east yard scheduled and knew it was going to be a big turnout. I knew the Kings were going to take advantage of this *rec movement* also, to talk about strategic warfare. It was going to be a major show of force on both sides between the Muslims and the Kings. It was inevitable but I prayed for now that no one would set it off.

Riiinnggg, sounded the bell, signaling the start of the recreation movement.

"*On the rec!*" shouted Officer Polaski, the guard on duty into the intercom.

As I rose from my bunk, I felt for the knife by patting my pants pocket. I thought for a moment, *what am I doing? If I get caught with this thing, I'll be spending at least six months in the box. If I leave it here, suppose I get jumped?*

Then I thought about the many years I actually carried an unlicensed handgun. I remembered how, whenever I was asked why, I would say, I would rather be caught by the cops with it, than to be caught by a mugger without it. I reached in my pocket and positioned the knife in a way, that when I grabbed it, the button would be under my thumb. It was no question now. I decided I would carry it with me whenever possible.

"I wonder if they cleaned up all that blood yet?" said Woody as he prepared to leave *on the rec* movement.

"Bilal," he said.

"Yeah."

"What's gawn happen between the Kings and the Muslims?" he asked.

"We'll see," I said.

We all spoke briefly after we came back from *chow* about an hour earlier. It was then Mr. Watts walked in and said a guy at his table told him about the blood on the walkway. Neither Rico nor I mentioned anything of my involvement. Watts worked in the laundry behind the state shop and hadn't been on the other side of the compound to see it.

"Don't tell me you goin' out in all that bullshit, Bilal?" said Watts.

I just smiled as I adjusted my *kufi* in a mirror that I had taped to my locker.

"Boy!" he said in a fatherly tone with his hands on his hips.

"I'll be OK," I said to reassure him, then turned and exited my cube.

Aw, man," he said complainingly, "you can't tell a Muslim shit. Y'all think y'all know every goddamn thing."

"Rico!" he called, "Tell him how dangerous them Spanish boys are," he said.

Rico just smiled as he reached for his fingerless, leather, weightlifting gloves from the top of his locker.

"Don't you know they planning a war behind that shit?" said Watts.

"Don't worry man, I'll be OK," I said as I walked past his cube.

"I need to tie your ass down to your goddamn bed and make you stay here with me," he said.

"I appreciate your concern, Mr. Watts, but picture that," I said laughingly while walking out.

"You just watch your back out there boy!" he yelled from his cube.

As I ascended the stairs, I had my hand in my pocket, nervously sliding my thumb back and forth across the knife's button. I looked up to see if my Muslim brothers were waiting as before.

To my surprise, "Bilal!" said Alim. He was surrounded by Muslims waiting on my behalf in the stairwell. "Let's go, let's go!" he said.

"*Assalamu alaikum*," I greeted them.

As I exited the building, I could tell something was different. A newcomer might not have noticed but something was different.

"Man, can you feel it?" said Alim.

"Feel what?" I asked.

"The electricity," he said.

"What?"

"The tension in the air," he said.

"Now that you mention it," I replied.

"Look!" he said and pointed to Muslims gathering at the fork in the road that led to the four dorms across the grass.

"Let's hurry up, they probably waitin' on you Bilal."

"Me?" I said and we all quickened our pace.

Congregating by more than six people was illegal, let alone stopping on the walkway. There were small groups of Hispanic inmates gathering also, and now even a *new jack* could tell something was up.

"What the fuck is goin on!" screamed a sergeant as he approached the group of gathering Muslims.

"Keep it movin!" he yelled. "Any shit outta' you guys and I'll turn this goddamn movement around," he said. "Come on, hurry up! You too Chico!" he disrespectfully directed to one Hispanic inmate who was slow walking waiting for friends to catch up.

It was obvious now that things were getting out of hand and the movement had just barely started.

"Bilal!" shouted Big Brother Malik.

He was in the center of the group. His height and size made him easy to spot. It also in return made me easy for him to find in the crowd.

"C'mon!" he yelled, and the small group of Muslims I was with stepped up our pace.

"*Assalamu alaikum*," I greeted Big Brother as I approached him alongside.

"*Walaikum salaam*, I want you with me. Brother Alim," he said, "I'm glad you're here.

"What's up?" asked Alim.

"Y'all packin'?" asked Big Brother.

"Yeah, I am." I answered.

"What about you?" he directed to Alim.

"I ain't limpin' 'cause I'm cripple," said Alim.

"Hahaaa, the slayer? I didn't think you'd show up without it. Man you nuts," laughed Big Brother. "You got heart, Alim," he said.

It was known amongst the Muslims that Alim had made a sword in the machine shop where he worked and on special occasions, he would make it part of his attire. This happened to be an occasion of such.

All of the *shirta* team and the *wazirs*, or heads of different detail groups, were mostly Muslim inmates who had showed courage or leadership qualities. Along with the *amir*, our spiritual advisor, they made up the executive branch of the community. All of the decision making was made by them in accordance with Islamic Law. The only other member of the executive branch was Imam (spiritual leader) Mustaffa Muhammad, a civilian spiritual advisor, or outside *imam*. He was in the facility only five days a week with an office and on the state's payroll as was clergyman of the Jewish and Christian faiths. Each major religious group behind prison bars has an outside clergyman on the facilities payroll and space enough for the inmate members of the congregation to worship. Since the death of our amir, Hassan on the day of the dogs, the community had elected Sheik Yusuf Ali (You-sef Ah-lee) to advise us in the ways of Islam. He, as any other older Muslim man usually over fifty years of age with graying hair, was called *sheik*, out of respect for the wisdom one acquires from his longer life's experiences.

Walking along side Big Brother gave one a feeling of strength and confidence and any inhibitions I had back in the dorm, were for the moment completely gone. There was a heavy presence of guards. They knew how to read the signs as well as any veteran inmate. They knew when there was going to possibly be static between the organized groups of inmates such as the gangs or the Muslims. All a *new jack* had to do to figure this out was to watch for the number of guards along the walkway. Now they were everywhere. Suddenly two state vans rounded the turn up ahead. They were slowly making their way through the movement of inmates with magnetized police flashers stuck to the metal roofs of each. This was a tactic they used often, whenever they felt there might be reprisals between two groups especially after an incident such as the one we had this morning. Alim was walking next to me and with every other step or so, we would bump shoulders caused by his limping. It was because of the sword he had concealed down his pant leg.

"Ok straighten up Zorro, here come the po-leece," I said to him.

"Zorro huh?" I'ma get you for that Bilal," he said jokingly.

When the vans approached us, we could see they were filled with guards. As they slowly rolled past, you could see on their faces that they were not too happy to be there. They knew what danger to themselves that being involved in the middle of a conflict between two rival groups entailed.

Shortly after the second van rolled past, "Malik! Malik!" a voice called from behind.

Big Brother stopped and turned around, as did the crowd of Muslims around him. It was our *amir,* Sheik Yusuf Ali. He was with another large group of Muslims not far behind us. We waited for the *sheik* before continuing our walk to the yard; we then continued to walk upon his approach. Sheik Yusuf, from Pakistan, was in his mid-sixties and fit as a fiddle.

"We want to see if these guys are willing to talk to us," he said. "That is best."

"Yeah OK," said Big Brother.

The *sheik* continued, "We want the man who transgressed and as many of their leaders as they feel safe to come to the *masjid* (mosque) on *Jummah* Friday.

"Yeah, go ahead," said Big Brother as he listened intently to the instructions given to him by Sheik Yusuf.

"We want the man to agree to receive one hundred lashes and to apologize to the community," he said.

"I got you," said Big Brother.

"With this, he should feel glad," said the *sheik.*

"But Sheik," said Alim, "What if he don't?"

"If he don't…" said Big Brother. "I want him personally, he added. "We gawn put an end to all their talk about who's runnin' this jail," he said.

"We been holdin' back all summer on their attempts to set it. It's time to get Islamic on they ass. Excuse my French," he said.

"Are we prepared for that?" asked the *sheik.*

"Oh, we're prepared," said Big Brother and patted his stomach below his waist.

"Well let's hope we don't have to resort to violence,

but we must get some recompense – that is our Law," said the *sheik*.

I knew now Big Brother was serious about the statement he made earlier concerning the axe being sharpened while we spoke.

"Bilal," said Big Brother.

"Yeah brother."

"Did you read what I told you?" he asked.

"I'm familiar with the passage," I said hesitantly.

"The men and I talked," he said. "Brother Alim, listen up! We nominated three new men for the team: Bilal, you and our young brother, Jihad. The kid got heart," he said. "Now you don't have to accept it if you don't want to. Not everybody's cut out for this kinda work. You'll have to live with your nightmares the rest of your life and there's always the risk of catchin' another charge, like manslaughter. Take a few minutes and think about it. Let me know when we get to the yard," he said.

"No question, I'm down," said Alim immediately.

Behind bars, *shirta* teams have been known to actually carry out sentences or bestow the appropriate, prescribed punishment on Muslims and non-Muslims alike in accordance with Islamic Law. I had proven myself in battle against difficult odds, but like a hangman or executioner, it took a special kind of person to fill those shoes. Islamic Law is based on issues far from turning the other cheek. Compensation from the criminal is paid to the victim or the victim's family by such things as sweat, possessions, money or blood and the punishment should equal the crime. In this case, blood for blood would have been an appropriate barter and what Sheik Yusef had suggested was mild in comparison. Lashes or flogging was only to be given upon consent of the criminal. Its primary function was to humiliate and embarrass, not to inflict severe pain. I, for a long time, wanted the prestige that came with being a member of the *shirta* team. It was a position that was revered by most Muslim men but now finally given the opportunity, I strongly felt that I didn't have the right stuff.

"Big Brother," I said.

"Yeah."

"It's an honor and a privilege to be considered for service under your command but I have to regretfully decline the nomination," I said.

Big Brother laughed, "Damn Bilal," he said. "We ain't in the army man, all you had to do was say no," he continued laughing, "You make it sound like I'm General Colin Powell or somebody."

"Yeah, don't you wish," I said, and playfully gave him a quick shot in the arm for teasing me.

"Look brother," he said, "don't feel bad. Only gangstas and fools take on this position in jail and I've never thought of you as a dummy."

"Brother," I said, "if you need a third man, what about Brother Jabbar (Ja-bar)?"

"He was our next choice," said Big Brother. "You tryin' to call him a fool?" he chuckled. "Oh, wait till I tell Jabbar," he said jokingly.

"You trying to call me a gangsta," I said.

Big Brother smirked. "Yeah right!" he replied.

This was the second week of July, and it was shaping up to be a hot summer night. The inmates were restless, and they were coming out of their dormitories in droves. By now, the entire jail knew of the situation between the Kings and the Muslims and those who would have normally stayed inside, came out to hopefully witness a gang war, firsthand. The *rec movement* ended with the *nine-PM go back*. It would be dark, a half hour before then, and if anything were to happen between the Kings and Muslims, it would happen then, under the cover of darkness.

As we rounded the turn past the medical building, vivid thoughts of this morning's life- death struggle between the King and I caused me to shudder momentarily. I wondered if this feeling of anxiety would haunt me each time I passed this now notorious landmark. It was only a few yards ahead that the crowd started to bottleneck slightly as the inmates made their way around the giant bloodstain. Still unwashed, still swarming with flies, it beaconed trouble: trouble that the guards were hoping for, so that they could finalize their investigation that would hopefully lead them to the dead Latin King's killer. I noticed ever so often, small groups of inmates would hesitate in front of the blood stain and ceremoniously make the sign of the cross. These I'm sure were mostly Latin Kings, sympathizers or very close friends of the deceased.

"There's a lotta Kings out here," I said.

"Who you tellin?" said Alim. He noticed it too.

"Look around you," said Big Brother Malik. "We Muslim strong out here. Let these fools play themselves. They'll catch a New York City Islamic beatdown," he said threateningly.

I smiled, then glanced over my shoulder. I was awestruck at the amount of *kufis* I saw behind me. It seemed as though Muslims who didn't own *kufis* borrowed them from other Muslims who had extras.

"Whoa!" I said, "Where'd all these brothers come from."

"See!" said Alim. "See how good we look when we all representin'. You ain't seen the half. Wait till we get to the yard!" he said. "When we hook up with the brothers from the south and east sides, we gawn be awesome!" he added.

As the long crowd of inmates before us made its way down the hill, I could see four guards on the catwalk of the east gate's tower, all holding high-powered rifles, ready to take action in the event of an uprising. When we reached the bottom of the hill, the programs building was to our right. Beyond that was the law library, gym and then the east yard. Already, one could see inmates forming groups of six, gathering in the field. They were positioning themselves far away from the structural recreation facilities. The basketball courts, handball walls and exercise weights area were all virtually barren...

As we drew near the gated entrance, the crowd came to a standstill as the guards checked ID cards before allowing entrance to the yard. I noticed there were no guards beyond the gate as they usually were.

"Ain't no po-leece out there," I said.

"Good," said Big Brother, "we don't want no state witnesses out here no way."

"They know what time it is," said Alim, meaning they knew better than to be caught in the middle of a clash between two rival groups.

"Brother Yusuf!" called Big Brother to the *sheik*.

He had dropped back a few yards to mingle amongst the large tailing group of Muslims behind us. Shortly after, Sheik Yusuf appeared on the other side of Big Brother.

"Yes brother," he responded.

"Stay close," said Big Brother. "Me, you and Bilal are gonna meet with these *kafirs*," he said. "We gawn let 'em know what's up, and we gawn tell 'em to back up off Bilal. They push-up on another Muslim, we gawn take some heads," he said.

This time, I didn't ponder over the validity of Big Brother's statement. I knew that the axe he spoke of earlier was now snuggly hidden below his waist. He was so large a man, that with his loose-fitting clothing, he concealed the modified axe, with very little effort. Later I was to find out that more than three quarters of its handle was sawed off.

While awaiting entrance to the yard, one could see through the gate how most of the inmates were there mainly as spectators. They looked like on-lookers at a major event, waiting for the entertainers to arrive in their limos. As we trickled through the gate, we were faced by crowds of inmates gawking curiously at the long stream of *kufi*-clad Muslims coming in. Realizing there were actually no guards in the yard itself, the inmates took the liberty of forming groups larger than six. Unrestricted in their movements, the inmates started grouping in larger numbers, the largest groups of course being the organized gangs. On the field were already the Muslims from the dormitories on the south and east sides. All wearing *kufis*, they were all sitting in the grass awaiting our arrival; it was a full turnout. I glanced at Big Brother. He was smiling proudly. He was second in command under Sheik Yusuf but these were his troops, and he was as anxious to greet and speak to them as we all were to be given an agenda.

As we neared the group on the grass, "*Shirta*, stay with me!" Big Brother cried out, and as our relatively small group of *shirta* members partially surrounded Big Brother Malik, it made me feel as though, maybe, I made the wrong choice by not accepting the nomination. It was an honor to be an official member of this intimidatingly formidable looking group of men, but I knew in my heart that I didn't have the right stuff.

As we came upon the first seated Muslim, *Assalamu alaikum*," Big Brother greeted a young Muslim who was a new transfer. "I'm Malik, *wazir* of *shirta*, what's your name?" he asked.

"John, I mean Abdul," said the young Muslim, as he stood up.

"Welcome to Mohawk," said Big Brother as he shook his hand. "You have any known enemies in this jail?" he asked.

"No, not that I know of," said the young man.

"Are you sure? You are tellin' me the truth?" Big Brother asked very seriously.

The young man thought for a moment.

"Yeah," he said. "No, I ain't got no enemies here."

"OK, my brother," said Malik. "If you do, just let me know and we'll take care of it. Add your name and where you lock to Amir Yusuf's list," he said, and the *sheik* stepped forth and introduced himself.

Big Brother continued walking toward the center of the seated Muslims, introducing himself as he looked for a place to make our base. Some who were *new jacks* were in awe of him and it was quite obvious that Big Brother Malik had a reputation that preceded him. They were sitting in no particular order and totaled close to one hundred.

"Young brother came in wearing a *kufi*," said Alim with a smile. "Look at all these Brothers," he said. "Must be getting' rough out there in the streets," he added.

Combined, we numbered almost two hundred, about fifty more than the previous week at *Jummah*. We had no idea of the number of Kings we had to contend with and regardless of the amount, they were still a formidable opponent. They had a reputation for being vicious, brutal and deadly anytime they were involved in an altercation, whether alone or as a group. The guards knew this too. I still felt it was an unwise decision for the facility to encourage such a potentially explosive scenario.

We followed Big Brother toward the center of the crowd.

"Hey Bilal!" someone called from my right.

It was Brother Habib (Habeeb). He was sitting in the grass about thirty yards away, holding up a small, traveler's, magnetic chess board that he always brought along with him to the yard. We played regularly together whenever we had the chance.

"I'll be back in a few," I called back.

"You can run but you can't hide," he cried out.

I stopped short and almost considered playing a game right then, until...

"Come on, Bilal," said Alim while pulling me by the arm. "That brother got you by three games already."

"Nah, man," I said. "The last two games were stalemates," I added.

"Come on step to your bidness. We got bigger fish to fry," he said. "And straighten your *kufi*," he added.

"Man, if you don't leave my *kufi* alone!" I threatened jokingly and continued to walk with the *shirta* team till we reached an open patch of grass near the center of the Muslims. This for now was to be Muslim headquarters. As we got situated in the grass, I observed first-hand the way the team functioned in an efficient and orderly manner. I watched how members of the other various detail teams reported in orderly fashion to their superiors, the teams' captains. They, who in turn, reported to the wazir of *shirta*, Big Brother Malik.

Most of these men were hardened criminals with a soft spot in their hearts that allowed them to be touched by the power of God's goodness. Compassion, courtesy, and kindness are not common attributes found among inmates and gang members. To them, they're generally taken as signs of weakness. Muslims in jail are rarely seen offending one another and when caught, are either reprimanded, punished or isolated. Compounded by a few factors such as virtually staying in touch constantly with God by praying five designated times a day and mandatorily praying once a week together on Fridays at *Jummah*, most Muslims in jail treat and embrace each other as true brothers, even at first introduction at times. Some of these brothers had taken human lives in the past and hideous scars were apparent on the faces, arms and hands of some of them from previous altercations in and out of jail. One such team member named Shahbaz

(Shabazz), housed in the south quarter; he was one of the team's captains.

"So my moms wasn't the only one who raised a fool for a son," he said smilingly as he approached Alim and I from behind.

I was sitting in the grass and Alim was lying on his side. We were both awaiting instructions from Big Brother who, at this time, was listening to reports from his captains.

As I looked behind me, "Brother Shabazz, what's up!" I greeted him.

Shabazz was a body builder and took his position as a *shirta* team captain very seriously. His face carried a five-inch scar from the bridge of his nose, across both lips, down to his chin.

"Hey brother, how you doin?" he greeted Alim and held his hand out to shake.

"I heard you brothers made the squad," said Shabazz as he reached down for Alim's hand.

"I declined," I said in a regretful tone.

"Your momma ain't raise no fool," he said.

"Well my momma did!" said Alim proudly.

"Well welcome aboard," said Shabazz as he stood shaking Alims hand.

"I'ma drop a jewel on you," he said, meaning he was going to give Alim some advice. "If a *shirta* officer approaches you, respect the rank," he said, "either sit up or stand. It shows eagerness to serve."

"Oh, I'm sorry, no disrespect brother but I can't sit down. I'm sorta like, strapped," said Alim and patted his thigh.

"Oh, you brought the dragon sword?" asked Shabazz excitedly.

Most of the Muslims had heard of Alim's prized piece of hardware.

"Yeah, the dragon slayer," said Alim, grinning with pride.

"OK listen," said Shabazz, "if we split the team up in groups later, I want you on my squad, cool?"

"Wherever I'm needed," said Alim, compliantly.

"Brothers, I got to go," he said, "I'll be back, Alim. If anybody asks you to team-up, tell 'em you wit me. Please!" he added.

"Alright, no thing," said Alim.

"Alright," Shabazz repeated. "*Assalamu alaikum*," he said as he left.

"*Walaikum salaam*," said Alim and I.

"Hey Bilal," said Alim.

"Yeah."

"I'm proud of you, brother," he said.

"Why?" I asked.

"Because you got the strength to say no."

"No?" I said.

"Don't get me wrong, I wanted this job more than anything else in the world. I ain't got nothing to lose. Half my life's been spent behind bars, so it don't matter to me. But you, you know there's a better life outside'a here. I don't know nothin' else. Yeah, I lived out in the world before, but it don't last long. I'll get a good job, tooling at some machine shop and then I start making silencers for guns and machine gun parts and repairing pieces for the mob downtown in Little Italy. It always gets me busted, and I keep comin' back— it's the story of my life. It's the lifestyle," he said. "The lifestyle is so smoove, I can't shake it when I'm out there. And then cause I'm dealing in guns, sombody'll offer me a contract to take somebody out. I'm talkin' bout gettin' paid! You can't tell a monkey not to eat bananas. Not me anyway once I start sniffin' that dope. The best place for me right now is behind bars and I know it. Allah put us all here for a reason and I feel I can better serve him on the inside, for now anyway. A brother once told me," Alim paused.

"He said, he who lives without discipline, dies without dignity. That bothered me. Before I go back out in the world next time, I wanna have some discipline under my belt and I'm too short to the end of my bid right now to get the amount that I think I need. Hey what can I say— If I catch another charge, so be it. I ain't ready to step off now no-way. I'll get home when I go home, he said. Allah is the best of planners," he added.

"Man, you a genius brother! It shows in your work. You put a patent on that knife, and man you talk about getting' paid! Your biggest problem is that dope. Tell your counselor you wanna take a drug program," I said."

"Man, I done been to *ASAT (Alcohol and Substance Abuse Treatment)*, *CASAT* (Comprehensive Alcohol and Substance Abuse Treatment) and all that (New York state-run alcohol and substance abuse inmate treatment programs). It don't help," he said.

"How you been stayin' clean in jail?" I asked.

"I've been stickin' with the brothers, makin' my five." he said.

"Well, that's what you gotta do when you get out. I had

a serious *Jones* (drug habit). That's what I do, and it works for me," I said.

Alim thought for a moment, nodding his head, "Yeah brother, I'm real proud of you," he said.

It seemed almost as if Alim didn't comprehend the simplicity of the suggested solution I had to his problem. Unfortunately, a large percentage of Muslims in jail return to their ungodly ways shortly after their release, and for Alim, that had obviously been the case in the past.

"See," said Alim, "you can even say no to drugs. Now that's discipline."

"No, that's a miracle," I said. "Some of God's work," I added.

CHAPTER 6

Takbir!

It was late in the day; the sun was casting long shadows and soon visibility in the field would be difficult in the fading light. Alim had fallen asleep in the grass, and I sat watching the movements of the largest group of inmates that had gathered not too far away. I tried to pass it off as a mild case of paranoia until I noticed one too many of these inmates stretching his neck looking in my direction. These were Latin Kings.

"Alim," I said while shaking his shoulder to wake him.

"Yeah!" he responded, then he quickly propped himself up on his elbows. "What's up?" he asked.

"I'm being eyeballed by these clowns."

"What?" he said.

"Kings, they checkin' me out," I said.

Alim turned his eyes toward the direction I was looking.

"That's a lotta Kings!" he said.

By now the sun was gone from the sky and the

surrounding grass had come to life with the sound of crickets serenading one another.

"How long was I asleep?" asked Alim.

"A while," I said.

"Did Brother Shabazz ever come back?"

"Not yet," I said.

"Man, they got a small army over there," he said referring to the Kings.

Most of the Kings were close to the weightlifting and exercise area. It was obvious that some of them were working themselves up, trying to prepare themselves for an upcoming fight. The body language told it all. Some would throw a barrage of punches, eagerly shadow boxing after a light workout routine. Suddenly we heard one of the brothers calling the *Adhan*; it was time for early evening prayer, *Maghrib*. It wasn't uncommon for Muslims in the yard to make congregational prayer at prayer time. The guards gave us no problem with this; it was our religious right. As the Muslims started to gather, most were stretching and loosening up their limbs from being stationary while sitting in the grass.

"I gotta sit this one out," said Alim.

"Don't worry," I said. "I'll put in a good word to the boss for you," I said jokingly.

With the sword hidden in Alim's pant leg, it would have been impossible for him to prostrate during prayer. As I stood up, Big Brother approached us.

"I need a sentry. Me and you Alim, we gawn stand guard while the Brothers are prayin'," he said. "You on one side and me on the other," he added.

Both Alim and Big Brother were well armed and

hopefully the Kings wouldn't try anything while the *ummat* (Islamic community) was vulnerable.

"Give me a hand, Bilal," said Alim, and I helped him to his feet.

"Bilal, I want you to shadow me," said Big Brother. "Stay close, after *Maghrib* we gawn talk to these *kafirs*," he added.

We assembled into four ranks of approximately fifty each. Out in front on both sides, were Big Brother on the left and Alim standing proudly on the right. Their sole job during prayer was to stand and watch for any danger while the rest of the congregation worshiped. I felt admiration for Alim; he was in his glory. Only a *shirta* member could hold the position of sentry, this was understood by the congregation. I watched how, whenever he was congratulated for making the team, he would humbly nod his head and smile. It was hard to imagine Alim, who worked so hard at trying to help his fellow Muslims keep up a good image, was the hell-raiser he claimed to be out in the world. After we made *Maghrib* prayer, the twilight of dusk was upon us.

"Bilal!" called Big Brother, then he turned and walk toward Sheik Yusif, who had led us in prayer.

As l stood up, Big Brother signaled to the rest of the congregation to stay down.

When I reached Big Brother and the *sheik*, "I've been watchin' 'em," said Big Brother.

Just then Alim approached the *sheik*, Big Brother and me.

"Man, they all over Bilal," he said excitedly.

Alim had been watching the Kings' activity also.

"I know," said Big Brother. "I don't think it's a good idea for Bilal to be with us, Sheik," he said. "Alim," he said, "tell the captains to get their men up front. Tell Shabazz I need him here with me."

"Done!" said Alim and left to carry out the orders given to him by Big Brother.

"Bilal, I might want you to wait here while we go talk to those fools," said Big Brother. "While we were prayin', they were doin too much pointin', and all eyes were on you.

Sheik," said Big Brother.

"Yes brother," he answered.

"You ever see so many brothers sportin' *kufis*?" he paused, "in jail?" he added as he looked out over the heads of some two hundred Muslims.

"I can't say that I have," answered the *sheik* smilingly.

"I know a lot of these brothers are scared," said Big Brother, "but after tonight, tomorrow they'll be walking tall." Big Brother took in a deep breath and exhaled as a man resigned to becoming a martyr. "We gotta show those *kafirs*, Muslim blood is sacred and Mohawk ain't the place to be puttin' your hands on a brother. We gawn make an example outta' somebody if they give us a hard time," he said.

The *sheik* nodded his head in agreement.

"What happened to the lights? It's getting dark out here," said the *sheik*.

It was then I realized that normally the flood lights that surrounded the yard, usually illuminated the field at this time. The facility was setting the stage for an imminent confrontation. It was getting dark fast and only the recreation areas were lit up. The only lights to be seen in the field were the fireflies blinking by the thousands.

"The guards know what's up, they tryin' to force our hand," said Big Brother. "Well, they gawn be puttin' in a lotta overtime. They gawn be up to their assholes in paperwork till daybreak if we set it off out here," he said.

I looked at the small army of Kings. They were repositioning themselves farther out into the field, away from the recreation area, and closer to us. "They movin'," I said.

Big Brother quickly turned around.

"That's their leader up front, Santana, the big guy," he said. "Funny, his brother is Rico, king of the Netas," he said.

"What!" I exclaimed. "Rico?" I said, "Rico's my roomie, he never mentioned that to me."

"Oh, you in *a penthouse*?" asked Big Brother. "Yeah, he probably spends a lot of time trying to forget that he has or even had a brother," he added. All dormitories had the same layout or floor plan in all of the buildings at this camp. No matter where you locked, every dorm had *a penthouse* and Big Brother understood the terminology.

"Yeah, but Rico's cool," I said, "How come they're on different teams?" I asked.

"Story has it that Rico took the weight for Santana in a dope raid and caught a *skid bid* (short state time) back in the day. Two years later Santana got busted in one of his own warehouses and turned state, saying that he worked for his brother already doin' time. They hit Rico with fifteen-to-life on top of his sentence and Santana walked. But see, God don't like ugly. Santana came in here three years ago on a trafficking charge, and if it wasn't for the King's, he'd be dead by now. A lot of these guys used to either work for him or shot his dope. They all think he's gonna put 'em on once they get outta jail. He'd pimp his own momma first," said Big Brother disdainfully.

Alim came back with Shabazz. The *shirta* team, consisting of about twenty men started to gather around us.

"Shabazz," said "Big Brother, "me you and the *sheik*, we gonna take a walk."

Shabazz answered with an affirmative nod of his head.

I had thought about taking responsibility for my own actions. The least I could do was to try and get no one hurt over something that I took upon myself to execute.

"Big Brother," I said. "I'd like to do my own bidding, I mean if it's alright,"

"You just as crazy as Alim; no wonder y'all always together," he said and smiled.

He looked at Alim standing next to me; he wasn't smiling. Instead Alim had a look of eagerness on his face, and you could tell he wanted in on the negotiations.

"Oh no, not you too," said Big Brother while looking into Alim's eyes that glared with excitement. Big Brother thought for a moment. "I should have never told you two to come," said Big Brother. "Come on," he said finally, "Y'all wanna invite anybody else?" he said facetiously. "Rookies," he said while shaking his head. "But rookies with heart," he added and smiled. Big Brother turned to Shabazz, "Ok Shabazz you stay with the squad. It's gettin' dark, we gotta move. If anything happens to me, Shabazz is second in command. Y'all know what y'all gotta do," he directed to the team. "Do the rest of the brothers know what the deal is?" he asked Shabazz, referring to the two-hundred-odd seated.

"I told the brothers, if they swingin' or look like they been swingin', to take 'em out.

They shouldn't be out this far no way," said Shabazz. "Not unless they Kings," he added.

"Good move," said Big Brother. "Tell the brothers to stay seated. I want *shirta* to wait at a non-threatening distance behind me. If you see us go down, set it off." he said to Shabazz. "C'mon," he said to Alim and me, and as the four of us, including the *sheik*, departed from the crowd, I recall swallowing hard to try to rid my throat of a lump that had welled up inside me from fear.

I didn't know what to expect. *Would they grab me and take me hostage?* I thought. *Hostage for what?* I concluded. These guys wanted my life and here I was giving it to them on a silver platter. I started to doubt whether I did the right thing by asking to be present at the confrontation with the Kings. I've got to do this. It's only right. Besides, I can't turn back now. I thought.

"I won't turn back now," I whispered.

"What?" said Big Brother.

"Nothin', I was just talking to myself," I said.

"You know what they say about people who talk to themselves," he said.

"You think I ain't?" I replied.

Big Brother smiled.

It was only about one hundred feet to where Santana had stopped at the forefront of his small army. I noticed he was flanked by what must have been his warlords and other high-ranking officers. I assumed this by their arrogant postures and the way they gestured commands to their now gathering troops. Three hundred strong were the King's army and as we drew nearer, the almost silent gathering became louder and more boisterous the closer we approached Santana. In the receding twilight, I noticed Santana was wearing a red bandana tied around his forehead. Unlike his brother Rico, he was a fairly large man in his late forties. Although younger, he wasn't a body builder like his brother. His sloped shoulders, slender arms, and slightly bulging mid-section showed signs of the proverbial good life. I saw Big Brother from the corner of my eye make an adjustment to the axe in his waistband, and I felt a rush of blood to my head and ears. The feeling of anxiety was overwhelming. Now, it wasn't fear I felt at all. It was the anger building up inside me. The mounting feeling of retaliation against that creep Loco, who could potentially grant me a murder charge and conviction or now, a ticket back home in a body bag. We were so close now. I wanted to reach in my pocket and palm the knife Alim had given me, but it would have been unethical to approach an enemy to negotiate peace with a weapon in hand; besides, we were too close for me to have made such a move and have had it gone unseen.

"That's close enough!" said Santana in a stern voice.

We were ten feet away, and you could tell in the semidarkness, that even the air around us was uninviting.

"We ain't here to fuckin' talk," said Santana angrily.

"Let's rip these fuckin' beanies," shouted one excited King standing behind him.

"I'm fucking talking here!" shouted Santana over his shoulder as he raised both hands to silence his men. He lowered his hands to his hips, "You got something to say big man?" he directed to Big Brother.

"We come in peace," said Big Brother.

"Yeah?" interrupted Santana. "Well, we didn't!" he snapped, then stood there laughing, encouraging more hostility toward us from his men.

"Look," said Big Brother, "I'm gawn make this brief," he said. "One of you clowns attacked a Muslim. You of all people should know the deal behind that. We talked about this once before a couple of years ago and this time we ain't takin no shorts."

As Santana stood with his hands on his hips, he turned toward his men grinning. Without a word spoken, he turned back around and seemed to be rehashing a past conversation with Big Brother regarding the consequences of attacking a Muslim. Santana folded his arms and started stroking the hair of his goatee.

"Let me get it straight," he started. "You want me to let you beat one of my men down like a dog," he said.

"No!" interrupted the *sheik* and took a step forward. "It will not hurt him," he said in his Pakistani accent, "It's just a symbolic gesture to the Muslim community to show he seeks forgiveness. It will be done with a dry towel."

Santana's attitude changed to aggression.

"Can't you see we're fucking Kings, old man! You can't whip a King like a dog," he barked arrogantly at the *sheik* while stepping toward him.

I noticed Alim flinch for his sword. "Back off him!" he said threateningly.

It was because of the reverence we all had for Sheik

Yusuf, and all hell would break loose if any harm came to him.

Santana focused on Alim looking him up and down. He looked back at Big Brother.

"Who's in charge here?" he asked.

"You talkin to 'em," said Big Brother motioning his head toward the *sheik*.

"The old man?" asked Santana. "Well look old man," he said and turned and gestured to a young man at the front of the crowd. "Loco!" he called and as the young man approached Santana, I realized even in the darkness that this was the guy who sliced up Abdul Latif and got away.

"Come here brother," said Santana and put a fatherly arm over Loco's shoulder. "This is one of my young warriors," he said proudly. "Now look old man. He is a King. Does he look like a dog?" he asked arrogantly.

"He looks like a misguided young man," answered the *sheik*. Loco looked at him venomously.

"Oh, fuck you pops!" he said in an enraged voice and spat in the *sheik's* face.

I hadn't noticed his hand behind his back, and as he raised his arm, I saw he was holding something in it. Fortunately, Big Brother was aware of it. Loco leveled his arm off at the *sheik's* head and in an instant, Big Brother had grabbed his wrist. With a sharp twist of his body, Big Brother with one hand had rolled Loco across his hip, spinning him like a rag doll down to the ground. With a loud bang, the zip guns mentioned earlier had now proven to be fact. It discharged with a bright flash the instant Big Brother slammed him to the ground. In that split second of light, I saw a still shot of Big Brother kneeling over Loco with his arm held high above his head. He was holding the fire axe by the handle with its huge blade only inches from his grip. Its handle had been cut short so it could be used as a cleaver. I was deafened by the blast, but not so that I couldn't hear the chilling screams of Loco's mournful cries of pain. I was blinded by the effect of the flash momentarily. I almost panicked when everything turned bright white.

For those few seconds, I realized I was being rushed by Santana's men, none of which could get a good hold of me as they bounced into one another in the chaos. It felt like high school football, like I was the receiver on a punt return, fading in the opposite direction of any touch to my body. I almost exploded into a blind run, then miraculously, as if I were a blind man given sight, I thought I saw something moving. All around me I could hear grunts and bumps; men pushing and shoving and the savagery of all out hand-to-hand combat. I grabbed the knife in my pocket, prematurely pressing the button hard, feeling a solid click in my tightened fist and ripping my pocket wide open as I hurriedly yanked it out. I dropped down on one knee, blinking my eyes franticly trying to force myself to see. It was like a civil war movie as the wave of Muslims coming from behind me were shouting and yelling as they came to our rescue. Fear of being trampled to death got me to my feet. The moment I stood erect I was accidentally pushed from behind by a Muslim brother and was sent stumbling into the midst of the King's army. Seconds later I wasn't the only Muslim to invade their space. There were *kufis* all around me. It was too dark to recognize faces, but the voice of Big Brother came through loud and clear.

"*Takbir!*" I heard him shout.

"*Allahu Akbar!*" I yelled, along with two hundred other thundering voices chorusing the same.

"*Takbir!*" he shouted again and before I could respond, I was charged by a non-*kufi*-wearing King with his arm cocked back like he had steel in his fist.

I didn't want to use my knife if this guy was unarmed. I strained to see his hand, so I could hopefully make the distinction. I waited too long. If it was to be steel in his hand, I made my move too late.

He had the clear-cut jump on me and would have beat me to the punch when suddenly, "*Allahu Akbar!*" screamed Alim.

He was right next to me all the time. With a terrific lunge, his sword caught the King mid stride, point first running him completely through up to his fist. The charging King's momentum carried the three of us backwards. We hit the ground hard, knocking the wind out of me as I landed on my back with the weight of two full grown men on top.

"*Takbir!*" shouted Big Brother a third time.

"*Allahu Akbar!*" shouted Alim and the others, and in an instant, Alim was up on his feet and suddenly charged another King wielding his sword like a swashbuckler gone mad.

I could barely breathe and had to forcefully take in small breaths of air until I could catch my breath. The King who charged me was still pinning me down. I felt his body convulsing as his muscles twitched from reflexes, like his body knew it was dying and each muscle wanted to use itself for the very last time. I rolled him to the side and sat up. I was shocked when I saw the Kings were actually retreating. The Muslims were moving them back and leaving a virtual carpet of dead and wounded Kings in their wake. This was war and people were dying. I started to pull my legs free from under the dying King's thighs and noticed only twenty feet away was a man standing behind another who was on his knees. Neither had on *kufis* and I couldn't figure out what was going on between them. It seemed as if the man on his knees was being choked from behind.

Why doesn't he stand? I thought. *Why doesn't he try to get away?* I questioned.

I couldn't take the chance of not investigating for if it were a Muslim in trouble, he would soon be a dead man. I quickly got to my feet and crept up behind them with my knife at ready. Only a few feet away, I stopped and was surprised to see that the man on his knees was Santana. It was clearly him as his red bandana reassured me. He was franticly groping for the wrists of his attacker, who was cursing him in Spanish. *I know that voice*, I thought,

"Rico?" I called softly.

The man stepped around, looked me squarely in the face and said, "It's okay Bilal, this one is mine. I send him to Hell where he belongs."

I stood there frozen for a few seconds and watched Rico resume the task of killing his blood brother with a choke wire. I started to run, to catch up with the battle and was headed for the heart of the activity when I tripped over someone's leg. I noticed he was wearing a *kufi* and lying face down. I rolled him over gently by the shoulder to see his face.

"Jihad," I said. "Jihad!" I called again, shaking him by the shoulder to get a response.

I rolled him over completely on his back and saw the other side of his face was darkened with blood. I felt for his jugular vein to get a pulse and my middle finger slipped into a gaping hole, moistened with blood on the side of his neck. He had been slashed with a razor and left to bleed to death during the heat of the battle. I lowered my face to his and tried to listen for his breathing. The screaming voices from the battle and the yelling of the onlookers prevented me from making an assessment. I looked down into his boyish face and watched the white of his eyes carefully while I took in a full breath and blew a short, hard blast of air into them. He didn't blink. This was someone's boy and now he was dead.

He's young enough to be my son, I thought as I knelt over him frustrated and angered at the thought of how worthless were the lives of men such as we behind bars.

"God help us," I said softly and sat back on my heels, drained of emotions, looking toward the battle devoid of enthusiasm.

All around me were lifeless bodies of men who among their last wishes were probably thoughts of wanting flowers at their funeral and a death sentence at their killer's trial. As I sat there sullen in the dark of night, I watched as the battle drifted farther away. I heard someone running behind me and jumped to one knee turning and drawing the knife at ready. It was Rico heading toward the onlookers; his mission accomplished. He passed without saying a word.

We have a lot to talk about, I thought. *Then again, how do you strike up a conversation with a man about the subject of him killing his brother?* I concluded.

I looked back down into the face of this poor child of God and thought, *maybe by some miracle he could still be alive. Maybe he did blink, and I just couldn't see it in the dark. If he's alive, maybe there's still a chance to get him to the infirmary on time. I could be wasting precious time right now just thinking about it.* I felt compelled to do everything in my power to save any spark of life, if it existed in young Jihad's body.

Get rid of the knife, I thought, and I stabbed the earth in the center of the pool of Jihad's blood, hoping to use it as a reference point to retrieve the knife at a later date. The blood splattered in all directions, dotting my face and clothes, anointing me with this, the most sacred of Allah's creations, human, in this case Muslim blood. I stood and carefully placed my heel on the butt end of the knife and lowered my foot to solid ground. Then I knelt with my knees firmly against Jihad's side and worked my arms under his knees and back. He wasn't a large boy, only weighing about one hundred and thirty pounds. I lifted him, cradling him in my arms headed toward the entrance gate, his lifeless body easily conforming to the rhythm of my every step. Then suddenly, as if God turned night into day, the field lights came on and I could see that the battle had managed to carry itself to the concrete of the recreation area.

The only ones left in the field were the dead, the

wounded and me. I was the only one walking. As I passed through the carnage of the unfortunate, I saw the body of Santana as it stood out from the rest. Almost as if he were making *salat,* such as a Muslim in prayer. He was in a kneeling position, face down, but with his arms outstretched at his sides. I felt no remorse for this man, for I could only envision him consumed in his arrogance. Nonetheless, I did hope for his sake that Allah had a better life planned for his soul. I took a few more steps and couldn't believe my eyes when I came upon a human hand covered with blood.

"What the hell!" I said and couldn't for the life of me figure out what had happened here.

I continued to stare at it, puzzling as it was, and stumbled over something in my path. I twisted my ankle almost dropping Jihad as I lost my grip on his outer leg. I limped a few steps, stabilizing myself and regained control of my lifeless burden. Before taking another step, I swung Jihad's legs to one side to check my pathway and felt a chill up my spine when I looked down to see my left boot smeared with blood and next to it, a low-cut sneaker. In it, a human foot, cleanly severed above the ankle. It had to have been done by an axe.

Big Brother, I thought. He had the fire axe, and I recalled seeing him with it as he subdued Loco. I remembered the chilling screams after the loud report of the zip gun. This had to be the aftermath, the work of Big Brother. I carefully stepped over this, what looked like a prop from a horror movie and continued my walk toward the gate. There were two bodies up ahead lying face down. As I passed the first one, I could see he was no older than the child I had in my arms. *Never making it through their teens, how could a society subject their children to such deadly conditions?* I thought. *These kids weren't even old enough to legally buy cigarettes, but yet a society, ancient in comparison to its youth, could only resort to this? Allowing this type of self-destructing wisdom? The killing of its children?* I pondered....

I was grief stricken, seething in inner turmoil, walking with Jihad in my arms and feeling distraught over a great loss. As I came upon the second body, I noticed a slight movement of his back. He was taking quick, short breaths of air, lying face down and clutching the grass in front of him as if trying to pull himself along. The last thing I needed to see at this time was another child in effect, fighting for his life. *He wasn't a Muslim or a friend. He's the enemy and he got what he deserved*, was my first thought. Then I noticed he was wearing one sneaker. *I looked for his other hand, but his arm was folded beneath him. This has to be Loco. He's still alive*, I thought.

Now I was faced with the dilemma of choosing which life I was going to try and save first. Seconds mattered now and I recall walking right past him, choosing Jihad to be the recipient of my efforts. I took a few steps more and stopped. I looked up and took a deep breath searching for strength in the conviction that what I was about to do next was the right thing. My eyes became fixed on Polaris, the North Star, as it glimmered in the dark blue sky of early night. I felt a bead of sweat run down my forehead and into my eye. I blinked hard to squeeze it away. Then I looked down into Jihad's face, his eyes open with the blank stare of death. I glanced at the wound on his neck, inspecting it carefully, my eyes searching for even a minute flow of blood that would indicate life, there was none. I sighed deeply as I dropped to my knees.

"I'm sorry Jihad," I whispered. "I'm sorry," I repeated as the field lights started to blur, tears streaming down my face. I laid him down gingerly, laid one hand on his chest and closed his eyes with the thumb and forefinger of my other hand. *"Masalama* (goodbye) my young brother," I said and left Jihad's body where I stopped.

I rushed back to Loco still angered at the death of Jihad. Without concern for any pain he was feeling, for it wouldn't be pain he would die from if he were to expire. I grabbed Loco by one shoulder and pulled hard, turning him over, exposing his handless arm. He let out a low groan as I sat next to him.

"Help me," I heard him say in a low voice.

"You'll live," I said in a disrespectful tone.

Never looking him in the face, I untied my boots while stripping them of their laces.

"Help me," he begged again and as if his plea fell on deaf ears insensitive to his request, it went ignored without me saying a word.

His hand reached slowly to hold his handless wrist.

"Move!" I said angrily and brushed his hand aside, grabbing his wrist and quickly wrapping it around several times with my bootlace.

I then tied a square knot to secure it. I reached over and grabbed his leg, handling it roughly as he moaned in pain before wrapping and tying it securely with my other lace. In less than one minute his life was now saved. It was too bad I couldn't do the same for Jihad.

"Thanks," I heard Loco whisper as I stood and stepped out of my boots.

He realized, although he was handled coarsely, he received the lifesaving help he needed.

"Don't thank me, thank God," I said to him as I turned and walked barefooted to Jihad's body.

Moments earlier when I looked up at the North Star, I was contemplating whether I should help save Loco's life. I had come to the conclusion to let him live and be subjected to a life of awkwardness and humiliation. It's what Big Brother also wanted. It was now I realized what he meant, when he told me to read *Surah: 5 Ayat: 33, the cutting off of hands and feet from opposite sides. That is their disgrace in this world and a heavy punishment is theirs in the Hereafter* (Quran 5:33). *Allah is the best of planners*, I thought.

As I walked toward Jihad's body, I tried to come to grips with the fact that I had just saved the life of one of the men who started this whole mess. The battle was still raging in the far corner of the yard past the handball courts. The fence just beyond them was one of two that surrounded the yard. Some inmates that found themselves trapped between it and the battle, decided to climb to safety. They realized only too late that the fence was not a safe haven, but an alibi for the guards who opened fire from the tower. At the range of approximately two hundred yards, I could still make out the tower as a black silhouette against the night sky. I noticed several flashes of light near the top of the tower, then a few seconds later I heard the rifle reports.

Pow, pow, popow! rolled the thunderous explosions

across the valley below us, but not before four inmates who were clinging to the fence only seconds earlier, were now gone from sight. They needed to fire no more. The warning was well heeded by the rest of the crowd.

This can't be happening. They're really shooting at us, live ammo, I thought. I looked at Jihad's body on the ground in front of me. It seemed so unfitting for such a young boy to be left for dead as the others, like trash littering the field. I knelt down to pick him up and resume once again the task of bringing him in from the field. He was in the same position I had left him, and it came as no surprise. As I stood with Jihad, positioning him for a comfortable hold, I noticed a single flash from the tower.

Twang! went the sound of a bullet as it hit the ground only a foot in front of me and ricocheted between my legs. As the bullet whizzed behind me, I felt stinging sensations on both of my feet from the dirt that it kicked up. Kapooow! went the report of the single rifle round that was fired at me. Bullets travel faster than sound and from the distance of two hundred yards, it took at least a couple of seconds to hear the report.

They're shooting at me! I thought as I listened to the blast echo off the mountain on the other side of the valley. It wasn't the first time in my life I confronted death at gunpoint and now nothing was going to stop me from completing my mission. If it be death, then so be it, I decided and hefted Jihad's body, getting a firm grip, then boldly started walking. I took a few steps more and saw another flash of light at the tower. They had fired once again. This time a bullet grazed my right thigh, causing me to flinch, almost dropping Jihad. I gripped him tighter and clenched my jaws fighting the burn of my wound. Kapow! went the rifle's report. Now I was angry and looked at the tower hoping to communicate to the guards through their powerful rifle scopes, the hatred I felt for them with my eyes.

"You gonna have to kill me," I mouthed to them as I continued walking towards the gate.

Suddenly the gate swung wide open, and a wave of gray-clad officers came barging through. They fired canisters of tear gas into the crowd forcing the inmates to scramble in all directions, all wearing gas masks and armed with batons. They kept their distance from the inmates, not venturing but so far from the gate. Off in the distance I heard sirens, a lot of them. I looked toward the direction of the east gate entrance that was next to the tower. Every now and then I'd glimpse the flashing red lights of what had to be ambulances from outside hospitals on their way into the prison compound. There was a steady stream of them pulling up as I could indicate by their sound. The tower guards stopped shooting and I assumed they were busy preparing to receive the convoy of medical units.

I continued walking with Jihad's body now sweat dripping profusely from my brow, washing away all traces of any tears. The fighting stopped also, and inmates started to huddle in groups, away from the still smoking tear gas canisters. I was focused on the guards, watching as they too huddled, looking like creatures from outer space in gray uniforms. All donning gas masks, it made them look as alien as they truly were to the inmates. I noticed as I got closer, a man in a dark suit without a mask, making his way past the guards. As he stopped in front of them, I saw he was holding a bull horn. It was the warden, the man responsible for not turning on the field lights. The man who provoked us to war, all because he needed a suspect in the death of a Latin King. By no means was I going to turn myself in. Like brother Shabazz said, Momma didn't raise no fools.

It was hard to understand the logic of the administration. Like how the warden felt it would be better to have a gang war with possibly multiple fatalities to hopefully bust somebody for the death of one Latin King. Regardless of how many other people got hurt in the process, it didn't matter. A long investigation would look better on paper and the overtime spent on it would guarantee fat pay checks in the weeks to follow. Whose life would it affect anyway? Only us, the inmates, the people at the very bottom of society. Our lives meant nothing, for we were expendable.

I watched the warden raise the bullhorn.

"I want everybody to stay where you are. Just do what I say, and I promise you, no one will get hurt," he said. "I want everyone to lie down on your stomachs, cross your legs and clasp your hands behind your head. Anyone standing will be shot," he added.

I thought we were the bad guys? He sounded like an armed robber making demands of his victims, paradoxically making him no better than us...

The inmates responded immediately to his demands. At this point, I think everyone was glad to see the battle end. The grass under my feet ended abruptly as I stepped on to the concrete of the recreation area. I felt it to be very warm, almost hot to the touch of my bare feet. The late evening sun left behind its signature on everything it touched.

The first ambulance arrived at the scene and as it pulled up to the gate behind the guards, I watched it make a U-turn and backup into the trap for easy access to the injured. All of the inmates were lying face down except me. I stood out like a sore thumb, uncompromising and in defiance of a direct order.

"You!" shouted the warden into the bullhorn. He was talking to me. "You, stop where you are!" he said.

All I could think of was getting Jihad to the ambulance. I had taken the stand to do this or die and was prepared to complete this small task, even if it killed me.

"Stop or we'll shoot," he said into the bullhorn again.

I was so close now. He really didn't need the bullhorn at all. No guns were pointing at me, so I continued to walk the last few yards. Most of the guards started pulling off their gas masks to get a clearer look at me, crazed and bare foot carrying a dead child. In some of their eyes, I saw shame and somehow it felt good to know, that at least some of these men were compassionate human beings. The warden had a look of puzzlement on his face as he lowered the bullhorn.

"Stop or we'll shoot," he said in a low voice from only five feet away. His eyes were fixed on Jihad's gaping neck wound and he seemed uncomfortable when confronted with the by-product of his executive decision. "Oh my God," I heard him say in a low voice as he stared into Jihad's lifeless eyes. He looked up at me as I stopped directly in front of him. "What's this?" he said.

"One of your suspects," I answered and heaved young Jihad's body into his arms. "If he's not young enough, there's plenty more where he came from," I said angrily then turned and limped to the nearest inmate, assuming the same prone position.

As I lay on the ground, I recall the almost unbearable heat of the concrete and the ants crawling across my face. Drawn by my sweat they came from all directions; it was torturous to say the least. I was the closest inmate to the gate, only fifty feet away. I watched for the next two hours as the paramedics sorted the dead from the living. There were so many critically wounded that they loaded them in the ambulances, some of them not yet stabilized.

"Who's hurt?" I would hear them ask as they passed back and forth stepping over us, searching for casualties.

My wound was examined by a paramedic who determined that it could be treated at the infirmary.

"Are you sure?" I asked him repeatedly. I would flinch intentionally every time he touched anywhere near it, hoping for at least an overnight stay at an outside hospital.

I saw one paramedic walk past with an arm full of linen. He headed out to the field in the direction of where the battle began. I could see him spreading sheets, like he was making beds. Every time I'd see a sheet unfurl, I knew it was another body. I didn't know how many of the Kings were armed with lethal weapons, but I knew there was barely a Muslim without one; Alim had made sure of it. Those who didn't have a chance to bury their weapons in the field would never see them again, as I'm sure they tossed them away by the time the guards opened fire with the tear gas. It came as no surprise when they rounded us up, we the injured, to be treated at the facility's infirmary, to see the many sheets that were spread over bodies in the field.

As I was helped up by paramedics and led to a state van, I counted twenty-seven. It was a long night afterwards and I can remember sitting on the floor at the infirmary, everyone in handcuffs— Muslims and Kings side by side trying to stay comfortable while waiting to be seen. There were wounded inmates everywhere. We were herded into the halls and lobby like sardines in a can then made to sit on the hard terrazzo floors and forced to lean upon one another for support. There were over one hundred wounded at the infirmary, with injuries ranging from flesh wounds and shallow punctures to the gunshot wound of my right thigh. The ratio of Kings to Muslims was more than ten to one; I was of the minority. Needless to say, although we were all cuffed, I did not get a wink of sleep until I returned to my dorm late the following morning. I was given a new pair of boots to replace the ones I left in the field. More than twelve hours later I was released after a facility doctor tended to my gunshot wound. It was a very shallow flesh wound so they patched me up and gave me wooden cane.

All movement was suspended 'till the facility could clean up its act and now walking back to my dorm, you could see house gang inmates working in the field and recreation areas, cleaning up the aftermath of this facility sanctioned massacre. It was lightly drizzling, and the gloom cast over the compound seemed a fitting setting for what had taken place there the night before. *Hopefully the rain would wash away some of the blood from the walkway and the yard*, I thought. The sooner all traces of this dastardly episode in Mohawk's history was gone from sight, the sooner the inmates could go on with their daily lives with some degree of normality. From where I stood outside the infirmary, one could see the east yard's field. Not a soul in sight, even the guards that were always visible were probably busy doing just as Big Brother had predicted: doing the vast amounts of paperwork that comes along inherently with dead men in jail. It amazed me to see how quickly the facility could clean up behind itself and make a horrific scene disappear when it wanted to. Although the twenty-seven bodies I counted last night were gone, I knew I would never be able to sit in the field and enjoy the sunshine in the same way again.

When I reached my dorm, I approached the door peering through the small window. It was a full house. I knocked lightly with my cane to get the guard's attention. It agitated me slightly when I saw it was Officer Humphrey and not our regular morning officer that opened the door.

"Hey kiddo!" he greeted me. "We made this morning's news," he said proudly.

"Hey kiddo?" I repeated, "I'm old enough to be your father. Why can't you just call me by my name or number?" I said while looking him in the eyes as I limped past him.

"Hey, I'm sorry man, I didn't mean nothin' by it," he said. "But you guys kicked their asses last night," he added smilingly. I continued to walk towards my quarters. "I just wanted to say thanks. You guys made me a hundred bucks. I had my money on the Muslims to win," he said.

All I could do was shake my head in disgust. The thought of these guards making bets on human suffering angered me, especially knowing that I was almost shot to death while they probably cheered from the sidelines. As I walked down the aisle between the cubicles, I noticed numbers twenty-eight and thirty-six had been packed up. All of their belongings were in large burlap feed sacks and their mattresses had been folded and tied. They were the quarters of Raul and Edmundo, the only two Latin Kings that housed in A dorm. *Good riddance*, I thought. Now I could sleep at night and move about the dorm without worrying about a King *TOS*, for now anyway. I didn't notice them at the infirmary and now assumed they were among either the dead or wounded that was transferred to outside hospitals.

When I entered *the penthouse*, my roomies were all relaxing on their bunks.

"Don't everybody cheer at once!" I said, knowing that my whereabouts had probably been the focus of conversation all morning.

"My man!" said Mr. Watts. "Boy!" he started. "I ain't prayed for nothin' so hard since I bought my first Cadillac. I done told you about fuckin' wit' those Spanish boys."

"Yeah, you told me," I said solemnly.

"Bilal, what happened man?" said Woody as he stood looking down at my torn pocket, the one l ripped open with the knife given to me by Alim. "Man, you need to rent a room at the infirmary, you be over there enough. Maybe you need to get out the Muslims; that shit's gawn get you killed," he said.

"No, it ain't like that," I said.

"Ain't like what?" said Woody. "Look at you man, you all tore up," he said concernedly.

I understood the way Woody felt and knew he was truly trying to be helpful.

"You just don't get out of the Muslims," interrupted Watts. "A man don't change what's in his heart just like that," he said.

"Oh Mr. Watts don't start confusin' things. Not now, please," whined Woody. "I'm tryin' to talk some sense into the brother," he added.

"Yeah, some nonsense," grumbled Watts, then turned and walked back to his cube.

"Bilal, all I'm tryin to say is that you ain't got to be risking your life to worship our Lord."

"You're right!" I said. "But if you believe what is written, you should be willing," I added.

Woody paused momentarily thinking about what I said to him, so I took the opportunity to step into my cube.

"Yeah, I guess you right about that. To each his own," he said. "You Muslims got some strange ways about you," he added while shaking his head.

"Yeah, but is all good," I said and smiled.

"So, what happens now?" said Watts.

"About what?" I said.

"So, what happens when one side kills up a mess'a niggas? They ain't gawn act like it never happened. They ain't gawn just forget about it," he said.

"No," I said, "and they ain't gonna forgive us for it either, but without Santana they ain't got enough wind left in their sails for us to worry about it right now."

"Santana!" exclaimed Woody. "They got Santana?" he asked very concernedly.

I looked toward Rico realizing I spoke too soon.

"Who in the hell's Santana?" asked Mr. Watts.

Suddenly Rico sat up on his bunk.

"He's a dead fucking King! We should kill all those motha fuckas!" he said loudly.

"Damn Rico, what'd he do to you?" said Woody.

"That piece a shit" said Rico, "me and my men we help the Muslims last night. We kill all those fucking Kings," he said proudly.

I was puzzled by Rico's statement and stared at him not fully understanding what he meant.

"Helped the Muslims?" said Woody.

"The Muslims don't need no help," he said. "That's some strong shit you talkin' man," he added.

"My men, they walked with the Kings last night, like they Kings too," said Rico. "And when I give the word—" At that point Rico paused and while flexing his elbow, motioned with his arm three sharp jabs, as if he were stabbing someone and smiled. "We do it quick and go," he said, "because the Muslims, they were going to kill us, they think we were Kings too," he said and laughed.

"You bullshittin'," stated Woody and looked at me, waiting for me to dispute such serious allegations.

I ignored their conversation completely in an attempt to distance myself from the incriminating statements Rico seemed to make light of.

"You hear that Bilal?" asked Woody. "I don't know what either one of you are talkin' about," I said.

"He said the Netas mixed it up with the Kings last night on the down low. Is that true?" he asked.

"I have no idea, I wasn't even there," I said

unconcernedly while getting a fresh change of clothes from my locker.

"Loose lips have been known to sink ships," said Mr. Watts. "Y'all talkin' bout that shit like it's alright," he said.

"Oh, it's okay," said Rico. "We have no more Kings in A dorm. I make sure of it," he said.

"Them two boys?" said Woody in astonishment. "You did them two boys Edmundo and Raul?" he asked in a low tone, referring to cubes twenty-eight and thirty-six that were now packed up.

"I had to clean my house," said Rico and laughed again.

I didn't doubt Rico's statements. After all, he was a man of integrity amongst the inmates and had no reason to lie. If anything, he was running the risk of exposing his guilt and setting himself up for retaliation by the Kings. I, on the other hand, was able to sleep easier at night, knowing there were no Kings in A dorm to worry about. As I sat on my bunk gathering my clothes to take to the showers, I was overcome by the weariness of my ordeal. I remember lying back to relax for a moment and hearing Woody and Rico still talking about last night as I drifted off into a deep sleep.

A week had passed without any repercussions from the outcome of the war. It was as if nothing had happened at all. As I encountered small bands of Latin Kings in my everyday whereabouts, all the while wearing a *kufi*, I detected not even the slightest hint of hostility. In jail, living in the now is stressful enough to make one hesitant in reacting on things to do with the past. However, their brothers would not be forgotten. With the high body count and heavy casualties on the Kings side, as long as Muslims and Kings lived together in Mohawk, retaliation was just a matter of time. I assumed this was the case, so I stayed mindful of the circumstances that led the Muslims and the Kings to war and my integral involvement.

CHAPTER 7

Déjà Vu

Between the New York City Lockups and the New York State prison system, I had been incarcerated now for almost a year and a half, and by now had seen and lived in a world far more dangerous than any shooting gallery or crack house that I ever had the displeasure of frequenting. Just knowing that I was due for a parole hearing in a few months seemed to make the time pass more slowly. The days grew hotter but fortunately most nights brought with it a restful sleep attributed to the soothing breezes of the cool, mountain air. Many-a-night, I lay in my bunk longing to be home. Thoughts of family and friends now more than ever filled my mind and would keep me awake for hours, long after lights out. I would lay on my bunk and actually allow myself to feel the joy of what it would be like walking through the gates into the free world as a free man. I recall one of these nights dreaming of just that, walking past the guards at the administration building, snubbing them as I took my undeniable walk to freedom.

It was such an exhilarating feeling that I woke up out of a deep sleep only to find, it was all just a dream.

I returned to work on the day designated by my medical pass. After being briefly welcomed back by the crew, it was back to business as usual.

"So, what's up with the leg wound? Can you work?" asked Diamond.

"Only if you say so," I replied jokingly.

"If you want to go back to your dorm, I'll write you a pass, it's no problem," he said.

"No, I appreciate it. It feels good to be back outside," I said.

"Good," said Diamond, "we gotta cut down those trees on Deputy Lape's property today. Can you handle it?"

"We'll see," I said, and the van proceeded to the giant water tank where we geared up with supplies and the machinery necessary to do the job. We drove from the water tank to Deputy Lape's house, approximately a quarter mile on the perimeter road of the compound. By lunch time, all the trees that stood precariously erect repositioned by the storm of a week ago, we had felled, de-branched and sectioned into pieces of manageable size. Diamond had stayed in the van the whole morning doing the crossword puzzle in the daily paper while parked in Deputy Lape's driveway. He was surprised at the amount of work that the five of us had done in such a short amount of time and promised that if we kept up the same pace after lunch, he would give us a day off sometime during the week. A day off meaning that we still had to report to work, but he would allow us to lounge around inside the water tower and take advantage of the exercise and cooking facilities at our own leisure. After eating lunch, Mel approached me with a very serious look on his face.

"I've been up all night," he said while removing his glasses to massage his eyes.

"Aw, man!" I said, "Not again, Mel."

My response was due to the fact that Mel had a reputation for being up all night while doing drugs.

"No, I ain't on that shit no more, I've been cleanin' up my act. I got a letter from my wife yesterday. Bilal, she ain't wrote me back in six years. I sent her a letter last week. This time I begged her to send me pictures of the kids and she did. She said, she hopes I ain't found nobody else and she wants me to come back home when I get out," he said.

"Well alright!" I said.

"Bilal, I love that woman with all my heart. I can't believe this shit is really happenin'. I go to the board tomorrow. If they let me go, I'll be home in two months," he said.

"I'll be praying for you brother," I said.

"I want to become a Muslim," he said.

"What!" I said astonishingly, I was astounded.

"I want to become a Muslim," he repeated.

"Why?" I asked.

"Because, I believe there has to be a God. All last night, I thought about my life, about all I've been through and what you taught me in our conversations about what God expects of us. And if there's been any goodness I've done in life, it's because of what my moms taught me about right and wrong. She was a good person, a Godly person, only she was fucked up by those drugs. I don't want to wind up like her, dead in an alley somewhere, leavin' my kids without a father; they've done without me long enough. I wanna come back home and I wanna come back home right. I wanna learn true right from wrong so I can teach my kids how to be good people and not fuck up their lives like I did. I want to teach them how to save their souls. They're seven and nine now, it's not too late, is it?" he asked.

"It's never too late my brother," I said and reached for Mel's hand, pulling him closer to embrace him.

I was caught completely off guard. The least of all things I expected from Mel was for him to be in search of God's Laws.

After we embraced, I said, "Come to *Jummah* on Friday at 1:00 PM. You won't be disappointed."

Well, Mel attended *Jummah* that and every Friday and Muslim services four times a week to learn the ways and practices of Islamic belief. He took on the name Jihad Abdul Ghaffar (Ga-far). Saying that the name Jihad would constantly remind him of the great effort he needed to put forth, in guiding his family along the straight and narrow path to Heaven. He told me that he had read that the only possessions of this Earth we can have with us in the Hereafter was our children and he was going to do everything humanly possible to never be separated from them again. Of the 99 epithets or attributes of Allah, Mel chose Ghaffar. The name Abdul Ghaffar means servant of the forgiver. He said he had to do this because his love for his wife meant enough to him to try and find reason for her infidelity. Once he realized that he was part of her problem, he could not hold her completely at fault without accepting at least some of the blame himself.

Mel was granted parole, and just like clockwork he left

Mohawk Correctional Facility on the release date suggested by the parole board. I remember it well. That day, we the outside lawns and grounds crew were now back to being a four-man team. We were cutting grass and trimming hedges on the free world side of the administration building, outside the gate. Mel was inside the administration building going through the formalities of release. Diamond traditionally let the crew landscape the front of the administration building anytime one of the crew members was released. He did this because he felt a person should have at least someone greet him on the other side of the gate. It was his personal contribution to the rehabilitation process, he would say. As we half-heartedly went about our work, due to the fact that there was very little to do, for we kept the front of the administration building immaculately manicured at all times. We watched the parolees as they came out and entered the state van, one at a time. The van trip to the public bus station was the last responsibility to the inmates Mohawk Correctional Facility had to comply with.

Out came Mel wearing a black *kufi* and a black suit with shoes to match, courtesy of his now regularly corresponding wife. She was now clean five years and gainfully employed. I didn't recognize him at first and honestly, I thought he was an *imam* applying for the facilities Islamic Spiritual Advisor position.

"*Assalamu alaikum*" I greeted this free Muslim stranger.

"*Walaikum salaam*, I'm gonna miss you Bilal," he said.

"Mel? Is that you?" I asked surprisingly.

"None other!" he said with a smile while making a 360-degree dance twirl, elated by his newfound freedom.

The crew went wild. It made us all feel good to see one of us leaving in grand style. Diamond was grinning from ear to ear not far away as Mel was bidding us his final adieu. He and I made eye contact and he motioned with his head toward a beautiful well-dressed woman and two children standing behind him.

"Don't forget to write. Now get outta' here before Diamond re-arrests you for fraternizing with the inmates," I said.

As he turned towards the van his eyes caught a glimpse of the delightful surprise Officer Diamond had waiting in store for him. It almost brought tears to my eyes to witness this very special, long awaited family reunion. I can still see in my mind Mel waving goodbye from the passenger window of their late model sedan.

Two months later, I found myself at mail call, shoulder to shoulder with other enthusiastic inmates awaiting their perfumed envelopes filled with words of love from their sweethearts. I had gone in front of the parole board two days earlier and was expecting an envelope with their response.

"Eighteen!" shouted the officer on duty.

"Here," I shouted resoundingly.

"Parole Board!" he said as I reached for the envelope in his outstretched hand. Everything got quiet. "Open it," he said smilingly as I stood there motionless knowing I held the confirming words of the parole board in my hand.

"C'mon open it, Bilal," egged someone in the crowd.

As I ripped the envelope open with my thumb, I saw the word *DENIED* stamped in bold red print and my heart sank to the very pit of my stomach.

"Dam *akh*, what did you do man?" asked the inmate standing next to me.

He saw it too and now everyone present knew my results.

"It's too long a story to make it short," I replied solemnly. "Plus, I didn't do it," I added, embarrassing as it was. I clenched my jaws in anger.

"Yeah, that's what they all say," said the CO and frowned. "Thirty-six!" he shouted, and I turned to make my way through the crowd back to my cube.

Seconds later, "I'm number thirty-six, but this is for Edmundo Flores!" said the recipient of the letter. That ain't my name, this letter ain't mine," he said.

"Oh, dass one'a doze niggas who got killed. They packed him up; he don't live here no more," said someone in the crowd.

"Give it here, that was one of my brothers, I'll mail it to his family," said another, who was obviously a Latin King just transferred into A dorm.

They're back!, I realized alarmingly.

As I walked down the aisle between the cubicles back toward *the penthouse*, I searched my mind, heart and soul for words of consolation that I so desperately needed at this moment. Struggling, just to make it from one second to the next, "Be patient, I told myself. You're a man, you're a Muslim…" It was an oath I made the very first time the reality of imprisonment overwhelmed my thoughts, and the painful anguish of solitary confinement was all that was left to living…

Allah is the best of planners.
And He makes no mistakes…

Printed in the United States
by Baker & Taylor Publisher Services